D1553053

WHAT PEOPLE ARE SAYING ABOUT
VEGAN TEENAGE ZOMBIE HUNTRESS

. . . .

"Just the right proportions of zombies, snark,
and regrettable prom fashions. Tastier than a bucket of brains."

- Karen Kincy, author of OTHER and SHADOWS OF ASPHODEL

"...a geektastic thrill ride you won't want to miss. Piñata, FTW!"

- Steve Holetz, co-host, The BoneBat Show

"Definitely a fan of Clarissa..."

- The Horror Honeys, A Book of the Week Review

"This was a really enjoyable book....
I'm probably going to read it again, it was that good."

- Damian Legion, cohost of Z.E.D.D. Radio

. . . .

VEGAN TEENAGE ZOMBIE HUNTRESS

© 2014 G.G. Silverman

ISBN: 978-0-9905452-1-7

Cover design and interior design by
Rocket Ranch Design + Advertising:
www.rocketranchdesign.com

Front cover photo credits
lollipop: © Istockphoto.com/StudioCasper
blood drip: © Istockphoto.com/Mafaldita

VEGAN TEENAGE ZOMBIE HUNTRESS

G.G. SILVERMAN

*For Bananas, the world's first
zombie-hunting, zombie-sniffing dog,
and for Buddy, who is getting
more fearless every day.*

VEGAN TEENAGE ZOMBIE HUNTRESS

G.G. SILVERMAN

1

I NEVER INTENDED to become a zombie huntress; I had only intended to protest prom, high school's last bastion of patriarchal society. I felt bad for the girls in my school, who flocked to prom like it was the second coming of Christ, complete with double-rainbows and unicorns. I would save them from all things prom: the spaghetti straps, push-up bras, and fuck-me pumps in candy colors. I'd save them from the horror of hair extensions, the tyranny of tooth whitening, and the stupidity of silk-tip manicures. I'd save them from the neon hideousness of fake-n-bake tans, and from the ultimate indignity, the Brazilian bikini wax. All this ending in the evening's most absurd moment, the deflowering of virgins by dumb jocks in the back of Daddy's old Beemer. Dear sweet Gloria Steinem, it's enough to make me gag.

I'd been protesting prom for weeks, standing next to the prom ticket table with a table of my own. My best friend Cokie, who's as quiet as she is loyal, sat dutifully beside me as I handed out my carefully-composed, Pulitzer-quality flyers, like "Prom and the Reinforcement of Stereotypical Gender Roles in Our Modern Society," and not to be outdone, "Prom and Its Effects on the Developing Female Mind: The Dis-ease of Mass Consumerism." I secretly slipped in some other flyers, like "Meat is Murder" and "Veganism and You: Fighting the Meat-Industrial Complex." I even included, out of the kindness of my heart, a recipe for my favorite vegan, gluten-free brownies. The best way to reach people is to bombard them while you have their attention, and hope that something, or *anything*, sticks.

But I wasn't sure if anyone was listening. I needed to be at prom, with my bullhorn and picket signs, telling my fellow womyn they had one last chance to redeem themselves and embrace feminism before it was too late. Even though there's nowhere I'd rather be on a Friday night than staying in, reading Simone de Beauvoir by the fireplace, and painting my fingernails black, I knew that being on the scene at prom would be my last chance to save souls. Except prom night did not go as I had imagined.

2

ON PROM NIGHT, I tried to act casual at dinnertime. I didn't want to openly admit to Mom and Dad that I was going to act on my agenda. They thought my protest was "cute"—*after all*, they said, *was prom really that bad?* I frowned at the word "cute"— a word best reserved for baskets of puppies, newborn bunnies, baby boa constrictors and LOLcats. Yes, Mom and Dad were pleased that I marched to the beat of my own drummer, but they never expected me to go all the way and make a stink at prom. Or maybe they did, and that's why they were scared. After all, look at what history teaches us: Joan of Arc started out as a simple peasant girl, and though she led France to victory, she was thanked for her efforts by being burnt at the stake.

I sat at the dinner table, eyes down in my soup, when Dad ambled into the kitchen from the deck where he had been grilling burgers—which he did almost *every* night, despite the near-constant drizzle that happens when you live near Seattle. Mom, a high-earning career woman and proto-feminist, had given up cooking a long time ago, so Dad took to the grill like it was his salvation, reasserting his manly-man status with 88,000 BTUs of heat, tongs large enough to earn their own zip code, and a lifetime's worth of charred animal flesh. His need for fire and meat was primal, harkening back hundreds of thousands of years to his Neanderthal ances-tors, who high-fived each other before each and every Stone Age barbecue. But the bottom line is that I, the family vegan, often fended for myself. I once tried cooking for the whole family, but nobody liked the tofu parsnip goulash I made. From then on, we went our separate ways—Dad retreating to the grill, Mom only nibbling bits of blackened meat before opting out by claiming fullness and/or a headache, while I resumed eating the politically correct and alternative foods of my own concoction.

Dad pulled out a chair and sat down beside me, plopping a tray of burgers on the table, its carnage annoyingly close to my personal space. "What'd ya make tonight, kid?" he asked, feigning interest in my soup. He lifted a burger to his mouth and chomped noisily, oozing bacon, cheese, and other vile greasy tidbits that threatened his sweatshirt with a menacing drip.

I rolled my eyes. "Dad, you know you really don't care, so why are you even asking?"

"I'm trying to make an effort at being engaged in my daughter's life. I really, really am," he said with his mouth full. "So why don't you tell me what you made? Pretty please?" He made sad puppy eyes at me.

"Fine. It's sprouted wheatgrass soup. Vegan, dairy-free, gluten-free. High in nutrients. The green color comes from the high chlorophyll content."

"Sounds…delicious. May I interest you in a bite of hamburger?" He held it up to my face. I pinched my nose and turned away, almost gagging at the smell. Ugh, he asks me the same question every time, and I know he knows the answer, so at this point, I'm sure he does it simply to torture me.

Dad continued his sarcastic assault. "Why are you vegan again? Wait, wait, don't tell me—"

"—The Meat-Industrial Complex!" we said in unison.

Mom breezed into the kitchen, looking super sharp in her navy blue power suit. She kissed Dad on the forehead, and did the same to me. Then she looked over my shoulder, and sniffed.

"Whatcha eatin'?"

"Sprouted wheatgrass soup. Want some?"

"Eh, no. Looks like…pond scum. Sorry, love."

"Want some burger?" Dad offered. A speck of mayo lingered in the corner of his mouth.

"Oh, hon, I'm kind of tired of burgers. Got anything else? What about salad?"

Like he would ever know what that was.

"Yup, there's some bagged lettuce in the back of the fridge. Have at it."

I stood corrected.

Mom rescued the forlorn package of lettuce and tore it open with delicate fingers, dropping some into a small wooden bowl. She splashed it with fat-free dressing, sat beside me at our cozy, round kitchen table, and smiled her best *CEO-of-the-Year / Mom-trying-really-hard* smile. Uh oh. The interrogation would begin any moment now.

"So, I heard it's prom night. Still boycotting?" She lifted a forkful of lettuce to her mouth and chewed slowly, watching me sideways with the eyes of a suspicious woman.

"I'm definitely *not* going."

Mom raised one of her signature bushy eyebrows.

"Well, I *am* going, but not to dance, only to stand outside…"

More skeptical looks from Mom. "Only to stand outside and…*protest?*"

Dad let out a low whistle. He and Mom gave each other *THE LOOK*, a knowing glance that meant, *uh oh, all hands on deck, we've got a live one here.*

Mom grabbed my hand. "Look, honey, despite your father's frighteningly average IQ, we are fortunate to have raised a smart young woman. And we are so grateful that you have strong convictions and are willing to stand up for them. But…"

"But what?" I asked, completely exasperated. I thought that my mother, of all people, would understand my feminist leanings.

Dad chimed in. "But we're worried that you're missing out on a critical moment of teenage life, a major American rite of passage. Feminist or not, girls all over the world would *kill* to have the life you have, and they'd *kill* to go to prom." Dad was using the word "kill" an awful lot, which made me nervous. "Look," he continued. "We're just worried that you'll look back on this night and regret it."

Mom nodded her head in somber agreement and squeezed my hand even tighter. "Are you sure you won't regret it, my little nonconformist bunny rabbit?"

"Mom, I'm absolutely, one hundred percent sure."

I had no idea how prescient those words would become.

LATER, Mom and Dad stood in the doorway with me.

I cleared my throat. "Keys, please? Because I really *am* going to do this, you know." And then I pleaded extra hard: "Please, please, please, please, *pleaaaaase?*"

Mom finally started leveling with me. "As you know, I've never been a nervous mother and have pretty much let you spread your wings and fly your whole life, to do whatever you think is right. I'm all for you standing up for what you believe in, but please stay safe. If I see your face on the news tonight, I'd really like it to be for the right reasons. You know, for winning a prize of some sort. Please promise me you'll keep out of harm's way."

"*Of course* I promise," I said. "I *never* get into trouble, remember? I am the perfect daughter, and can say so without irony."

"Haha," Mom said as she patted me on the back, then dropped the keys to her trusty old Volvo into my outstretched palm. "I don't care about perfection, I just care about safety. It's a mother's worst nightmare to get a call from an emergency room. Luckily I haven't had to cross that bridge yet."

"You *definitely* won't. Thanks, Mom!" I hugged her ecstatically and kissed her on the cheek.

"Be careful out there, kiddo," Dad piped up over Mom's shoulder.

I turned and bounded down the front stairs to the driveway, where I loaded my freshly painted picket signs into the Volvo's trunk and slammed it shut with conviction. I slid into the cool worn leather of the front seat, closed my door, and waved goodbye while smiling my best *I'll-be-fine* smile. My parents waved back, with a look of both misty-eyed nostalgia and subtle worry. Silly parents. *I really will be okay,* I thought. I was about to start my mission, and hit the road for Cokie's house.

I HAD KNOWN Cokie Morimoto just about forever—since first grade, to be exact. Cokie wasn't her real name, but an unfortunate nickname given by a bunch of mean kids after she snarfed Coca-Cola out her nose all over Taylor Coletti's cake at his unlucky thirteenth birthday party, prematurely blowing out the candles with sugary brown nose-water. Though I tried to talk Taylor out of being mad, he never spoke to her again—or me, for that matter—and the rest of the kids teased her without mercy. She's been stuck with her nickname ever since. But, at this point, she doesn't seem to mind. She's good-natured—*so* good-natured she does whatever I need her to do, which makes her the best kind of friend you can ask for. Easily pliable with no discernible agenda of her own, she's a willing disciple and supporter in all my educational initiatives.

There was the time she let me dress her in a fuzzy pink rabbit suit splashed all over with fake blood, during my "Fur is Freaky" campaign. I attached plastic toy meat cleavers to her suit to heighten the sense of horror. It was utterly spectacular in its artistic perfection, even if I do say so myself. Regretfully, she was sent home by the principal that day. But sometimes you have to sacrifice for your convictions. And Cokie readily sacrificed for mine.

Then there was the time she stepped into a smiling gray dolphin costume to help me spread the word about the evils of dolphin slaughter. The kids at school swarmed us while making dolphin noises because they think we're annoying, but Cokie didn't flinch once. I swear that girl is the best.

Truthfully, I worried about Cokie a lot. Since the day of the Coke-Snarfing Incident, she spoke less and less, and when she did, she sometimes stuttered. When she wasn't with me, she spent most of her time locked in her room playing video games. I often wondered what went on in her head. Had video games taken over her brain, numbing it to the joys of the outside world? What kind of thoughts simmered in those eyes, cleverly shielded by a shock of jet-black hair, draped to avoid eye contact at all costs? Whatever was going on, she had withdrawn from life, possibly depriving the world of a special hidden genius.

I pulled up to Cokie's house. Her mom kept the front yard manicured in a peaceful, Zen garden kind of way; her dad's police car was still in the driveway. I beeped my horn to lure Cokie out, lingering on it for dramatic effect. I didn't want us to be late, after all. Cokie's mom opened the front door and waved, then started to approach my car. She wore a dirty red apron, like she had just been cooking. I rolled down my window as she came over, though I was getting nervous, worried that she'd drag me inside. I didn't want to be rude, but I also didn't want to stick around too long socializing. I was a woman on a mission. Feminism just couldn't wait.

She leaned into my car window, and pushed her chin-length black hair behind her ears as it fell in front of her face.

"Hi, Clarissa," she said, her gray eyes smiling and crinkling at the corners. "You eat supper already?"

"Yup, I did. Got a belly full of my own soup. Green soup. Lots of phytonutrients. Mmmm..." I rubbed my stomach in a circle, because it was funny.

"You sure you don't want food? I made vegan udon, just for you." Mrs. Morimoto widened her eyes and pursed her lips, looking hopeful that I'd come in and eat *her* soup. She always made an extra effort to make it vegan when she knew I'd be around—even though Cokie's dad preferred the non-vegan kind, and would jokingly grumble about it, albeit really loudly. But I almost always ate her soup, well, because it was delicious. I sighed. I really loved Cokie's mom and didn't want to insult her, but I absolutely wanted to hit the road. Like, *now*.

"Aw, I'm really sorry, Mrs. Morimoto, but I'm super full. Plus, we really, really have to go." I made the most regretful face I could, to show her how truly sorry I was that I couldn't stay.

"What is so special about tonight?" she asked, her expression curious.

"Cokie didn't tell you?"

Her face fell. "No, she doesn't tell me anything anymore."

"Don't worry Mrs. Morimoto, we're going to do something cool. We're protesting prom!" I smiled so hard I practically felt the corners of my mouth touching my ears.

She furrowed her brow, shaking her head. "Prom? Tonight is prom?"

"Yup!"

She scrunched her face even more. This wasn't the reaction I was hoping for. I could tell she had so many questions, but didn't ask; or maybe she thought we were doing the wrong thing and was too polite to say so. Meanwhile, Cokie emerged from the front door, wearing baggy black skater pants with a black hoodie, her black bobbed hair masking her eyes, as usual. She slunk toward my car as though she didn't want her mom to notice, then scooted around the side of it, opened a door, and slid into the passenger seat.

"Esther, you wear too much black," her mom said, using her real name. "Wearing all black means you are *mo ni fukushite*. In Japanese, it means *in mourning*. You look like you're going to a funeral." She shook her head again.

Cokie slunk down further into her seat and didn't say anything, then turned her face to look the opposite way out the window, ignoring everything her mom said.

Then Mrs. Morimoto leaned in close and whispered in my ear. "Probably good for you girls to go out. Get Esther away from video games for just one night."

"Mom!" Cokie's head whirled around.

"Okay, sorry, sorry..." her mom put up her hand in a conciliatory gesture. "You girls be safe."

"We will," I said.

Just then Cokie's dad came out in uniform, a dashing, slim figure in his police blues. He rushed over to my car and leaned in, resting one tanned arm in front of my window, while wrapping the other over Cokie's mom's shoulder. "Hey, it's our two favorite teenage girls!" he said, flashing bright, white, shoulda-been-a-movie-star teeth. "What's on the docket for tonight? Studying? World domination? Demon-slaying? Huhhhhh?" he winked. "Tell me, I want to hear all your great plans."

Cokie's mom turned her face toward his. "They're protesting prom tonight," she said, still completely bewildered.

"What?!" he said. "Protesting prom? You girls—excuse me, I mean *women*—are like feminist samurai, which is amazing because, we, the Morimoto family, have samurai in our blood. We are honorable fighters!" Then he leaned in and whispered, "Plus, seriously ladies, prom is totally dumb. You are doing the right thing. *Punch it in.*" He made a fist and held it up to me, and I bumped my fist against his, then he shot his arm into the car for Cokie to bump hers too. She raised her arm in a limp fashion, and bumped her fist half-heartedly.

"Whatsa matter?" he said to Cokie.

She shook her head. "N-nothing, Dad. It's...nothing."

"Well, if you don't wanna talk about it, at least don't make me say that teen girls are moody because that is a wicked stereotype and I don't wanna go there," he winked at me again.

I stifled a snicker. Cokie cracked a smile, then pursed her lips together, trying not to laugh. Her dad could melt through *anyone's* icy armor.

"There's my girl," he said. "And there's my favorite smile. Alright, you ladies kick ass out there tonight, yeah? I mean that only figuratively though, I don't need any more trouble than what I handle on a nightly basis down at the precinct. Tonight I'm on convention duty in downtown Seattle, though. Government folks. Should be a piece of cake, if not totally boring." He snored, pretending to fall asleep on his feet. Then he turned to kiss Cokie's mom, saying, "Bye, honey." He stepped away and waved as he walked to his car. "Good night, ladies!"

We all waved back. Cokie's dad was so cool. A *total* rock star.

Mrs. Morimoto leaned in again, admonishing us with steely eyes. "Ok, I really meant it when I said be safe tonight."

Cokie let out a long sigh. "Mommmmmmmm!"

"No worries, Mrs. Morimoto, we've got this totally under control," I said.

She nodded, then forced a tight-lipped smile as she stepped away from the window, standing back to let me drive off. "Be good!" she shouted as we pulled away.

I waved out the window and grinned back. *Of course we're going to be good. Don't you worry one bit.*

I was glad to finally be alone with Cokie, so I could go over my game plan one last time—my blueprint for converting girls into diehard feminists, getting them to ditch their prom gowns and follow us, like Pied Pipers of Awesomeness.

"Hey, hey!" I said. "Ready to carry out our mission?"

Cokie mumbled something barely intelligible.

I sighed. "What's wrong?"

She shook her head.

"Look, I know you're bummed at your mom, but are you mad at *me* for something? Fess up, what's going on? Come on, tell me. We're about to go into battle, and we need to be on the same page. We need to be a team. More than that—a well-oiled machine."

She shrugged, and turned her head to face out the window again, not willing to confess if she was angry or not. We would probably spend the rest of the ride in silence. Oh, well. Who needs conversation when you can have minions?

My car snaked down the winding, tree-lined roads of our mostly uneventful suburban town as we began our journey towards our school, Redvale High. Prom was being held there this year, because last year's darling prom-goers trashed the local, fancy-dancy, three-hundred-dollar-a-night hotel. Well, "trashed" is an understatement. The truth is, someone poured gasoline into the sparkling cider fountain, then someone else set it on fire, and the resulting *boom!* from the Fountain of Fire made sure my peers were barred from holding prom anywhere nice from here to eternity. This year, they were resigned to decking out the high school gym as best they could.

When we pulled up to the school, taffeta confections of every color were already tumbling out of limos, with barely-concealed breasts spilling out of gowns like over-filled ice cream cones. Orange faux-tans graced the limbs of both boy and girl, and bleach-white teeth grimaced under the blinding glare of flash bulbs. *Disgusting.*

I parked the car with military precision, we pulled out our picket signs and bullhorn, and marched proudly to the entrance, where we'd stand in support of our message. We were ready for whatever the night would bring. My hair stood on end with excitement. I couldn't wait.

3

PROM-GOERS BEGAN filing past us, arm in arm. I raised my sign, shaking it in the air with pride. I gripped my bullhorn with my fierce feminist fingers and bellowed slogans like, "Prom is for mindless consumers!" and "Prom steals your soul!" and my personal favorite, "Prom makes you preggers!" Cokie stood by me, waving her sign, both bearer and witness to my message.

Early on, we got only a few disgruntled looks from students passing by on their way into prom, and a couple of snarls, and some choice words like, *"Die, bitch!"* muttered under minty fresh breath. I had expected more anger from my peers. In fact, I had expected downright mass hostility. But as the procession continued, most of the students took on a glazed, faraway look in their eyes. So it *was* true. Prom really *was* turning their brains to mush. The damage had been done. Some also walked with a slight limp, or a shuffle. It was hard to see, but it was there. I shrugged it off as sports injuries, the industrial hazard of those with too much leisure time on their hands, like cheerleaders and football players. But I didn't care. I kept shouting, hoping that my message would break through the prom haze that was poisoning their minds. Then I saw *her*. My evil nemesis, Lila Logan, marched toward us with all the determination of a freight train.

Lila and I were diametrically and diabolically opposed. She was the editor-in-chief, lead writer, and all-around news slut for the Redvale Rag, our school's very own contribution to the scandal-loving cesspool we call Mass Media. She was the Spawn of Satan. The Sultana of Sleaze. The Starlet of Suckup. She was willing to do *anything* for her idea of a good story, which involved shame and derision in both print and blog form. She had been dogging me for weeks, pouncing on me in the least dignified of places, like when I had my pants down in the locker room, or the ladies' room. And she was about to corner me now for an "interview," I was sure of it.

Her long blonde spiral curls bounced in time to her steps as she marched. She was in full prom regalia, with a sugary pink gown the color of bubblegum, from which a bountiful bosom overflowed. False lashes fluttered on her eyelids like enormous black butterfly wings. Sticky pink gloss frosted her lips in sparkles. And she crowned all of this with a twinkling tiara that would make most queens blush. She was flanked by her prom date, as well as her two usual goons, Camera Boy and Sound Dude, who wore the vacant downcast expressions of men who'd had their souls beaten out of them. I mean, I'm a feminist, and even *I* think that's cruel. She stopped inches short of me and thrust a microphone into my face.

"Tell us about your latest *initiative*, Clarissa." She lingered on the word *initiative* as though it were a delicious poison, bad and good all at once.

I gritted my teeth. "You know what I'm doing, Lila. Geez, you've been after me like a heat-seeking missile for ages. Shouldn't you take the night off? You know, for *prom?*"

"A good story *never* takes the night off. *And*, in the pursuit of a good story, I'm just curious to hear if anyone has joined your cause?"

It was true that no one had, except for Cokie. Lila was set to embarrass me publicly, to put my epic failure online for all the world to see.

"They'll come around," I said, mostly to convince myself.

"Oh, *will* they?" she smirked. "I *bet* they're going to regret not having joined your cause. I bet they'll regret it for the *rest* of their lives." She opened her eyes wide in mock horror, and threw her head back, laughing—the way witches and other evil women do in the movies when they need to make a point. Then she waved at her goons and hissed. *"Turn off the camera, this is strictly off the record!"*

She leaned in until our faces practically touched. I could see the Vizined whites of her eyes and I was sure I'd be christened by angry flecks of spittle any minute now.

"Listen up, Little Miss Fun Hater. *Off the record,* if it wasn't for our school's strict but smarmy anti-bullying laws, I would bitch-slap you into next summer. If you ruin my prom—a moment I have been waiting for all my life—I am *never* going to let you live it down. Because I am running for prom queen—if you haven't already noticed my pre-emptively worn tiara—and if you ruin that for me, there will be trouble. After we graduate, I will hunt you down and harm you. Do you understand me, little bi-yatch?"

If she did bitch-slap me, I'd bitch-slap her right back, but I resented the word *bitch* and all its familiar forms, as it was degrading to women and dogs everywhere. Plus, I was practicing *ahimsa,* or non-violence, as Gandhi once did. So I just stood there, unmoving in stony silence. I didn't want to gratify her need for attention and control.

"One last thing, Fun Hater." She looked me up and down with a sneer. "Why do you dress like a beatnik every day? Wait, wait—I get it. Yeah, you think you're a little cooler than everyone else. A little different. *Special.*"

"No, I'm just—"

"Exactly what is going on here, ladies?"

I whirled around, startled by the voice of my favorite teacher, Mr. Harrison. He was my Philosophy and Ethics teacher, and the last person I expected to see at prom—not to mention that I had a hot and totally inappropriate crush on him. In class, I pretended not to notice the way oxford shirts stretched across his broad, toned, just-out-of-grad-school chest. I pretended not to notice the fit of his khaki pants as he turned toward the blackboard. And I pretended that the sight of his strong, manicured hands didn't send me into fits of delirium as he handed back our tests. During those moments, I struggled not to stare into his blue eyes and beam messages of love into his brain. So I would l hold my breath and stare at my desk as he walked past. "Nice job," he would say, as he dropped my test on my desk. *Nice job.* I would hang on those words all day, scribbling them in my notebook like lovelorn girls often do. *Nice job, nice job, nice job!* And now he was here, at prom. I thought I was going to die.

"Clarissa, I'll only ask once more. What is going on?" Mr. Harrison demanded.

Lila smiled and shifted her attitude from catty to cake-batter sweet as she cut in. "Oh, Mr. Harrison! Thank you so much for stopping by. I was just practicing my right to free speech here."

"So was I!" I wasn't going to let her get away with this. Not in front of my favorite teacher.

"Ladies! Enough. Whatever is going on, it's over. Clarissa, you can protest prom quietly—emphasis on quietly—but you can't get in the way. And you, whatever your name is..."

"Lila. My name is Lila."

"...Lila, then, please call off your goon squad, and please, *please*, just go enjoy prom."

"Toodles," Lila smirked at me and blew me a kiss as she walked away. She waved to her boyfriend and flunkies to come along. Then, from about ten feet away, she turned toward me one last time, silently mouthed the word "bitch," and continued on her merry way into prom.

I felt as though I'd been punched in the gut and had the breath knocked out of my body. My cause had been made a mockery of. And the last words Mr. Harrison said to Lila? *"Just go enjoy prom."* I thought that of all people, *he* would understand. I hoped right then and there that a piece of space junk would fall out of the sky and crush me into oblivion. Anything to put me out of my misery.

"Clarissa? Are you okay?" Mr. Harrison put a hand on my shoulder.

My mouth went hot and dry, and a huge lump bloomed in my throat. I couldn't speak, so I simply nodded.

"Ok, well, I have students to chaperone, so I had better go inside," he said, and half turned toward the school building.

"But be careful out there, I'd hate to see my star student get in trouble, ok?" Then he turned toward Cokie, who seethed silently by my side this whole time. "Keep an eye on her for me, will you?" he winked, and walked away, joining the last few students and chaperones heading into prom.

4

AS WE WATCHED the stragglers, Cokie turned to stare at the last couple going up the stairs. It was Connor Zhou and his prom date, Asha P., who wore a brilliant magenta satin dress with small, tasteful capped-sleeve shoulders, her normally wild hair tamed into an up-do. I had never seen her wear a dress before, and stopped for a second, my mouth agape. I was momentarily derailed from my mission, forgetting to shout my slogans. Cokie quickly turned away, as though she couldn't take it anymore, and we were left standing outside with our sagging picket signs, forlorn and deflated. I felt like a failure. I hadn't converted a single soul. Cokie hung her head low, downcast like a dog locked outside a butcher shop. I needed to cheer up, for her sake.

I put my hand on her shoulder. "Don't worry, Cokie. It'll be okay. We have to be strong if we want to win this war. The night is young. Who knows how it could all end? Maybe it'll be the two of us for the win after all." It was dorky, but I often used video game references to get her attention. And if I described this situation as a war, she might just get what we were up against.

Maybe everyone just needed time. Maybe by the end of the night, they would realize what a horrible sham prom was, and leave in droves. I imagined the girls tearing at their hair extensions and rending their clothes, Greek-tragedy style, and shaking their collective fist at the sky. *Yeah.*

"Come on, let's go see what's going on." I yanked Cokie's sleeve and dragged her inside. We wandered down the hall and snuck up the back stairs to the upper track that circled above the gym. We stood in the dark and watched in anonymous silence as the couples below danced a slow, awkward ballad, bodies close together. Candles flickered in the dim light, casting a warm, magical glow. Most of the girls had already kicked off their heels, but looked radiant in their silks, and the boys handsome in their tuxes. They looked so *romantic.* Like, *sweaty-palms* romantic. I felt a pang go through my heart. Had I been wrong about prom? Was I missing out on the greatest night of my life? Would I regret this forever? Would *I* be the one shaking my fist at the sky?

I heard Cokie snuffling softly beside me.

"What's wrong, Cokester?"

Cokie wiped her nose on the sleeve of her sweatshirt. "I…r-really…w-wish…I could g-go…to prom!" she stammered between sobs.

I spun to face her. "What?!"

"You…h-heard…me."

"I did. It's just that I've never heard you say more than five words this whole month!"

"That's…because…you…n-never listen!"

"That's not true! I totally listen!"

"Name…*one* thing…I h-have said…all w-week," she sniffled.

I wracked my brains, but try as I might, I couldn't think of a single, solitary thing. What she said was true—I hadn't exactly been keeping up on all things Cokie. I needed to make this right and show her that I cared.

"I'm sorry, Cokes. I really am." I felt truly horrible, and tried to sound as sincere as possible. "Well, I'm listening now, if it counts for anything. Please tell me, if you could go to prom with anyone in the world, then who would you have gone with?"

She stopped snuffling and wrapped her arms across her chest, like she didn't trust me with the innermost secrets of her heart. Her face hardened, as if to say, *"Don't go there."*

"Come on, who? I am *dying* to know."

She shook her head, and her long bangs shook with her.

"Please? I'm trying to be a good friend. *Pleeeeease?*"

She shook her head again, this time furiously.

I needed to up the ante. I needed to speak her language. "I'll buy you a video game for your birthday!"

At first she looked suspicious, but then her face relented a little, as though she might consider my offer. But it was clear I needed to sweeten the deal.

"How about this: I'll get you a video game for your birthday *and* one for Christmas, *and* you can teach me how to play your favorite zombie video game *and* I'll dress up as your favorite cosplay character and go with you to Comicon. Huh? Wouldn't that be coooooool?"

Her face relaxed a little more, and she smiled a sheepish grin. Then I heard a faint whisper:

"Connor...Zhou."

Connor Z. The kid who walked past us on the way into prom, who turned Cokie's head. He was a B-boy, a tall, skinny Chinese-American kid who could break-dance circles around the sun, and used funny words like "dope" and "fly." He *was* pretty cute. But I wasn't going to admit it out loud. Instead, I had a different question, one that cut to the core of our friendship.

"If you wanted to go to prom so badly, then why didn't you say something?"

Tears streamed down Cokie's face.

"B-because...I was afraid."

"Afraid of what?"

"That y-you would hate me...and not be my friend anymore!"

She started sobbing seriously now, and the weight of what I had done came crashing down on me. The one person who loved me the most, out of anyone in the whole entire world, had also felt she couldn't trust me. I was an awful friend. I was self-centered, manipulative, and only cared about my own agenda. Maybe Lila was right. Maybe I *was* a bitch. I was very, very sorry.

It was clear to me that this night was officially over. I had failed in every possible way. I could take Cokie home, and if she wasn't too mad at me, she could teach me to play zombie games as soon as we got there. That was the least I could do.

I gave her a hug. "I'm really sorry, Cokes. Come on, let's go to your house."

WE BEGAN OUR glum descent down the back stairs from the upper track, with Cokie staring at her black Converse Chucks as they squeaked on the stairwell. When we reached the bottom, she ducked into the bathroom. I swear that girl had the weakest bladder on this side of the planet. But maybe she had the right idea. I stepped in after her and took a quick break myself, darting into one of the gray stalls. I finished my business fast, trying not to breathe in the lingering odor of long-gone cigarettes, stale urine, and vomit-inducing hairspray fumes, but Cokie was still locked in her stall, tapping her toes and taking her time. I washed my hands, fought the urge to lean against the grimy, graffiti-covered wall, and waited, shielding my eyes against girl-bashing messages where I'd inevitably see my own name. Messages like, *Clarissa is cray-cray!* And, *Clarissa Hargrove is whack!*

"C'mon, Cokes. Hurry up. This school is getting old real fast. Geez, are you playing games on your phone in there?"

"No, j-just wait, already!"

I was pretty sure she was lying, but it didn't matter. I owed her some time to herself, I guess. "Fine, I'm going to wait in the hall," I said. "These bathrooms sketch me out."

"Fine."

I stepped into the hall again and noticed Taylor Coletti, wearing his signature camouflage jacket, standing by the gym doors. Taylor was the same kid whose birthday cake Cokie ruined years ago, the day the three of us became social pariahs and went our separate ways. Since then, he ended up being one of the Generics—a non-descript, moderately smart kid who hung out with other non-descript, moderately smart kids: not good-looking or wealthy enough to end up in our school's social elite, not ace enough to get into a top school like Harvard, just a plain kid who got pushed around from time to time—until he started wearing camouflage, which gave him a tough-guy vibe, an aura of untouchability that he never had before. It was also rumored he'd gotten into drugs. He and his crew kept to themselves, except for the last few weeks, when he seemed to wander the halls alone, standoffish against anyone and every-one, giving off a toxic vibe. I watched him take industrial-sized zip ties out of his jacket pocket and wind them around the door handles, effectively securing them shut. My heart raced. What was he doing?

"Hey," I called out, attempting to keep it cool as I walked in his direction. "What are you doing? What's with the zip ties?"

Taylor rushed at me. I gasped as he smacked his palm against my chest and pushed me into a corner, my head slamming the wall. He pulled a gun out of his pocket and placed the icy barrel to my forehead. "Just shut up or I'll blow your brains out," he hissed under his breath. It reeked of beer, the cheap kind kids stole from their dads and drank in the woods behind the school when they thought no one was looking. "Why aren't you in there with the rest of those prom assholes? Oh, wait, I know you. Yeah—you *hate* prom. What a *crazy* coincidence, because I do, too. Great. Because I'm about to make you an offer you can't refuse. If you help me tonight, I won't kill you."

"Help you *what?*" I squeaked, trying to hide my shaking.

"God, you're dumb, aren't you?" Taylor said, keeping his voice hushed, motioning off to the side with his free hand, pointing at something he hoped I'd see. "Poor baby. All those straight A's, and you still have no clue about anything at all."

It was then that I spotted a freakishly large, camouflage-patterned duffle bag on the floor. It was open and loaded with what looked like ammo. Next to it lay a large black weapon, some kind of semi-automatic rifle. It looked terrifyingly real, and deadly. I realized with cold horror that Taylor planned to mass murder everyone at prom, without regard to who they were, or what they did. We were all about to be leveled like daisies under the Grim Reaper's lawn mower. And in death, the students of Redvale High would all be made equal: prom kings and band geeks, jocks and geniuses, skaters and bookworms, gamers and gossip queens, sluts and stoners. My stomach churned. I fought the urge to be sick. I couldn't believe this would be the end. No, I needed to talk him out of this, gun to my head or not.

"Don't do this, Taylor. The kids in that gym may be sheep, but they really aren't bad people. *We* are not bad people. What have they done to you that's so bad?"

Taylor paused. I noticed his eyes were red-rimmed, like he'd been crying earlier. And they were glazed, like he was on something more than just cheap beer. And his scruffy dark hair looked greasy, like he hadn't washed it in days.

"It's not they, it's *she*."

"She who?"

"Christie McIntire."

I shook my head. I wasn't used to keeping up with every last person on our school's unspoken VIP list.

"You don't remember her? Blonde, nice rack? Hot, but not *too* hot—not enough that dating a guy like me would raise too many eyebrows?"

"What did she do to you?" I could feel my voice growing smaller.

"Duh, Genius, everyone knows. But maybe you've been too busy saving baby seals to follow the gossip. She dumped me two weeks ago and started fucking some college guy, who's here with her tonight. That bitch was only using me to cheat on tests." His voice shook.

"So you're going to kill everyone because of one dumb prom?"

He clenched his jaw, narrowing his eyes like he had more to say, but wouldn't tell me the rest.

"It's not just that, is it?" I said, somehow staying focused as I tried to talk him away from the proverbial ledge.

He shook his head. "It's everything," he spat, pressing the gun to my head even harder. "It's the social climbing. It's the fact that I'm not super brilliant and not special, and maybe I'll never be anything more than who I am right now, and who I am now right now pretty much fucking sucks. My mom left and my dad doesn't give two fucks about me. I'm smart but I may never go to college. I'm fucked. You hear me? Totally fucked. And Christie? Maybe she was the only bright spot in my shitty life. But whatever. You don't care. Your mom is a big shot at some big company, and your life is all set."

He stared me down, his brown eyes locking with mine as he clenched his jaw again. That's when I realized Taylor was just like anyone else, a kid who wanted a second chance but was stuck in his own echo chamber, hearing nothing but his own angry noise. And he had never been a bad kid, until now, when his thoughts were spinning out of control. If he went through with his horrible plan, he'd forever become a villain, his face plastered across the news, and no one would ever know or care about the real Taylor, some kid that had been bullied and pushed too far.

Taylor licked his dry, cracked lips, and continued speaking. "Well, whether you decide to help me or not, I've jammed all the cell phones so no one's calling 9-1-1." His voice got louder. "And I've secured every outside door in this building, and the gym doors, so there's no way out. I'm sorry." Taylor paused. "No—that's wrong, I'm not sorry. This place sucks donkey balls and I'm tired of the social climbing. I'll be happy as a pig in shit to see everyone go. Including you, Princess."

Taylor started babbling incoherently like a strung-out sociopath, the drugs taking their toll. I remembered that Cokie was still in the bathroom, and prayed that she would fall asleep there, or that she'd hit her head on a towel dispenser and be knocked unconscious, or that she'd flush and be miraculously transported to an inter-dimensional realm connected by a vast network of toilets, *anything* to keep her from walking out and becoming part of the shooting gallery. I cursed our luck as I spotted her creeping out of the bathroom, which, from my angle, was now behind him. Cold sweat dotted my forehead. She froze for a moment as her eyes met mine, and put her finger to her lips as if to say, "Shhhh." She continued creeping as Taylor blathered on, stopping in front of a blazing red fire extinguisher. I watched her struggle to lift it off the wall in painstaking silence. I pretended I hadn't seen her, and stared Mr. Crazy Talk straight in the eye. He pulled the gun away from my head and began gesticulating wildly with it. I felt the pit of my stomach drop to my knees, which became weaker with every passing second. But then Cokie—miraculous little Cokie—swung the fire extinguisher from behind, smacking him squarely on the head with a resounding *clang*. He landed on the floor with a dull thud, his pistol flinging to a dark corner of the hallway with a clatter.

It was over. I closed my eyes and breathed a sigh of relief, my whole body wanting to collapse. My mouth felt like cotton as I attempted to speak. "Nice job, Cokester," I said. "I was hoping you'd never leave the bathroom, but now I'm glad you did."

I threw my arms around her, and felt myself crying. But our love-fest ended as fast as it started, because Cokie pulled away in a panic.

"We sh-should t-tell a teacher or someone!" she said, dropping to her knees by his limp, lifeless body. She bent down and lowered her head above his face, turning it so her right cheek hovered directly above his lips.

"I don't feel him breathing!" she hissed.

"What?!"

"I think we killed him! I m-mean, I think...I think *I* killed him. Oh m-my God. *Oh God, oh God, oh God!*" She grabbed his wrist, about to search for a pulse.

But just when we thought things couldn't get any weirder, the music died, and screams slashed the night.

WE RUSHED TO the gym doors, and peeked through the small windows. A chill fell over me as disaster unfolded before us. The slow-dancing crowd had degenerated into a scrambling, angry mob. Previously handsome boys now had sickly, blood-smeared faces and vacant eyes. They launched a frenzied attack on anyone in their path, wrestling their prey to the floor to gorge viciously on flesh. Girls who once looked angelic became wild, biting and clawing anyone in reach, spilling blood on their designer gowns as it dribbled down their chins. Even the chaperones joined the cannibalistic fray, chasing their quarry like hungry wolves. The rabid crowd of monsters moved quickly, driven by an insatiable need for people-meat. Others ran screaming from the horde until they were cornered and mobbed. We jumped back as some managed to reach the gym doors, and pounded on them only to realize with horror that they were locked in—seconds before being torn down right before our eyes. More monsters rushed the doors, heaving against them with the full weight of their bodies, hoping to get us next.

We backed away farther, reeling from the insanity. Cokie turned to me and gasped the most surreal words I'd ever heard:

"Oh, shit. *Zombies.*"

Zombies? Oh, shit.

Zombies. The Z-word. Ambulatory meat robots. Soul-less, brain-munching automatons. Snarling, sniveling flesh-eaters. A vegan's worst nightmare.

My mind churned over the scene. It was a horror movie made real, and even though I've never watched a horror movie in my life—I believed them to be the cinematic equivalent of junk food—I was pretty sure that no amount of them can ever prepare you for *this*…whatever it was, a true zombie outbreak or not.

The gym doors stopped rattling as some of the monsters scrambled away, while others dropped to the floor to eat their kill. I ran back to the doors, suddenly remembering that Mr. Harrison was among the chaperones. I scanned the room through bloody windows, hoping to catch a glimpse of him and find out if he was alive. I didn't see him. Where could he have gone?

"Taylor jammed the cell phones," I panicked. "We can't call 9-1-1. We're doomed, unless we find a way to break out of here and run. Can we smash those zip ties on the back door? Or that big window, can we smash it? That's it, we should smash a window!"

Cokie looked at me, shaking uncontrollably. "Wh-What about Connor? We can't just leave him!"

"Cokie, we don't even know where he is. And if we don't leave now, we're screwed!"

Her eyes went wide as more screams wailed in the distance, except this time, the screams came toward us from a different place.

"Oh, no," Cokie moaned. "No-no-nooooo."

I looked into the gym again. Zombies pushed through a set of doors on the opposite side, on the front end of the school. Taylor must not have secured them. And monsters moved out through the locker rooms, too. They were all just down the hall, and it would be sixty seconds before they found us, on the back side of the gym. They were coming *this* way, *right now*, driven by the juicy delicious smell of *us*. My blood curdled. We really were screwed.

7

COKIE RAN TO the corner of the hall and scooped Taylor's pistol from the floor, tucking it into her pants like she knew what she was doing. Then she grabbed an old baseball bat from a pile of dusty gym equipment in the corner by the exit.

"What are you doing?" I screeched.

"Just t-trust me!" She yanked my hand and dragged me towards the bathroom, where she jerked the door open and pulled us both through, keeping us behind the door.

"This is crazy. What are we—"

She clamped a hand over my face to shut me up, until she was satisfied I was done running my mouth off, then let go and handed me the bat. I nodded hard and held my breath. She cracked the bathroom door open and pulled the pistol from her pants, holding it like she was ready for an ambush as she peeked outside—though I had no clue if she was holding it the right way. In a flash, the screaming and snarling got louder and closer, but came just so far until we heard the sound of bodies smacking into the double doors in the hall—the ones that separated this hallway from the next one, the hall that led to the locker rooms.

Boom, boom, boom, went the doors. *Boom, boom, boom, boom, boom.*

"No one's b-breaking through," Cokie whispered. "They c-can't open the double doors."

A shiver ran up and down my spine. I peered over her shoulder so I could see, too. I felt sick as I watched a girl being ambushed against the doors. She screamed as she slid to the floor, fingers trailing blood down the windows as the freaks dragged her down. We heard them ripping into her body and jostling each other for the best angle, the best spot to get a taste of a prom girl. My gut clenched. It was the most horrible thing I'd ever seen.

"Why didn't the doors open? Did Taylor lock them?" I whispered.

"I d-dunno. Stay here, I have to t-try something," Cokie whispered.

"What?! Where are you going?" I tried not to panic as Cokie darted out of the bathroom, running past Taylor's body toward the double-doors in the hall. She stopped right before them and knocked, trying to get the creeps' attention.

She jumped back as they popped up from where they were feeding and lunged toward her, crashing against the doors that stood between them. She flinched each time the doors smacked, and my stomach lurched in time to the noise, but they held shut. The creeps couldn't get through. We were safe, at least for now.

Cokie ran back to where I was, and threw her body behind the bathroom door. "I got it," she said.

"Got *what?*"

"They... they're on the wrong side of the d-doors. They c-can't pull open, they can only p-push."

"Huh?"

"W-whatever's happening to them makes them really d-dumb...they don't understand how a door works anymore. All they c-can do is try to run at something...and if it opens under their body weight, they k-keep going. If it doesn't open, they t-try to bang on it but they d-don't know how to pull the handles...or twist a knob. If slamming on the door doesn't work, they t-turn around...to look for the next thing."

"So...so that means if we stay here, they can't get us, right?"

"Not through those steel doors. Even if they p-push their hands through the little windows, they c-can't get much farther."

I slid to the floor, pulled under by a tidal wave of relief, and passed out.

I **WOKE UP** with Cokie kneeling beside me on the cold, dingy gray tiles. She shook my shoulders gently, trying to snap me out of my fainting spell. In my mind I cursed our janitors for never getting the floors quite clean, and I cursed my bad luck for being there, butt-down in their sloppy work. But then I remembered that I had bigger things to deal with: the fact that our school had gone crazy and we might be in a fight for our lives.

"Geez, you f-freaked me out. I was afraid you'd n-never wake up," Cokie said.

"Sorry, it's just that this whole thing is so crazy, my brain couldn't take it anymore."

"I know. You should try to d-drink some water or something."

I groaned as I attempted to stand, sore from where my tailbone had hit the floor. Cokie got up first and grasped my arm, hoisting my body up next to hers. The faucet handle gave a shrill squeak as I turned it, and I dipped my head under the spigot, letting a stream of cool water flow into my mouth. Cokie did the same at the next sink, and when we were both done, we faced each other.

"Just *what* is going on out there? I know you said zombies, but, *really? Zombies?*"

Cokie shook her head. "I d-don't know for a fact. But I can't explain what's going on any other w-way. I think it's some k-kind of sickness."

"It's just not possible…maybe it's some crazy party drugs

that all the kids took…"

"If it was d-drugs, then the teachers wouldn't b-be sick."

"Then if it's some kind of virus or disease…then how come we're not sick?"

"I don't know. Maybe we're n-next. Anything c-could be making people sick…food…water…oh my gosh, we just d-drank the water!"

I felt like my head would cave in on itself. I thought about what all of this could mean. That maybe the folks at our school weren't the only ones suffering from crazy people-eater disease. That maybe everyone in the world was infected. Maybe my mom and dad were sick too, tearing each other apart at home with more than their loving, well-meaning barbs. I started to snif- fle… no, full on tears streamed down my face, burning my skin with their intensity. I felt the strength leave my body again. I stopped caring about the grimy floor and sat down, miserable. "Oh no, maybe my mom and dad are in trouble," I moaned.

"Maybe mine t-too." Cokie sat down beside me, also crying. "I w-wish I was home."

It dawned on me that if it weren't for my stupid ideas, we wouldn't be here; instead, we would be home, safely in the comfort of a living room or bedroom. I'd be studying up for finals while Cokie would be playing whatever game she could get her hands on. And it would be cozy, and just fine, better than this God-forsaken, high school zombie hellhole. "I'm sorry," I said. "If it weren't for me, we wouldn't have to witness this horror show. This is all my fault."

"No...no...that's not...t-true. If it weren't for you...I'd b-be in there...with Connor...maybe...I don't know."

"So...you're not mad?"

"No."

"You should be," I insisted.

"Nope." Cokie shook her head, her hair swinging from side to side.

I let out a small laugh through my tears, the kind you make when you've just witnessed some absurd horror and can't believe you lived to tell about it. We sat side by side, each of us lost in thought, trying to figure it all out.

Soon, we stopped crying, and I looked at my watch. "It's been a few minutes at most, but it feels like we've been here all night. What are we going to do?" I whispered. "Do you think we can call someone now?"

Cokie struggled to pull her cell phone out of her pocket. "Still n-no signal. Taylor's cell phone j-jammer is still working. My d-dad says that they're illegal, but cops and FBI can still use them, t-to interrupt terrorists and stuff, b-because terrorists use cell phones to t-trigger bombs. But you can still get them on the b-black market...."

"*Damn.* Damn that Taylor. Damn him all to *hell.*" I slapped the floor. "Well, at least he didn't use his cell phone to trigger a bomb, that freak, because that's pretty much the next thing

I would expect from a low-level terrorist. Which is basically what he is, at this point." Sarcasm dripped from my voice. I was starting to feel punchy. No, I was more than punchy—I felt like a caged animal that had been poked into a rage. I decided right then and there that I wanted to get out of there, and I would do whatever it took.

"So, listen up. We need to blow out of here."

Cokie didn't respond. Sadness flickered across her face.

"What's the matter? I know it could be scary out there, but it's better than staying in here, right?"

She still didn't utter a word. Her eyes held heavy thoughts, things she wanted to say, but couldn't.

"Well, spit it out, Cokes. We haven't got all night."

"No," she said quietly.

"No? What do you mean?"

"I mean, I want to stay."

I couldn't believe my ears. "Why on Earth would you want to do that?"

Cokie looked down at her feet. I knew that look. It was one of mistrust, and I had seen it so many times tonight. I felt bad.

"Come on, Cokes, *why?*"

She hesitated before answering. "Connor," she said quietly. Her eyes teared up again.

"I know you like him, but he's probably a zombie, or whatever those creeps are. And if not, we could kill ourselves trying to find out. This is crazy talk, pure and simple. Really, you have taken the last train to Crazy Town."

"So?"

"So? It's *so* not worth putting yourself in harm's way for a guy that's not your boyfriend."

Cokie became quiet again. I needed to strong-arm a sane decision. "Well, fine, you can stay here and try to save your prom crush, but I'm leaving. I'm breaking out of here all by myself. Don't forget, I'm the one with the car, so if you stay here, you're *screwed*. Plus, have you forgotten? There are brain-munchers out there."

"Fine, whatever," Cokie said. She had stopped crying, and her voice had taken on an edge of steely resolve. "Then go by yourself. I'm staying."

"Ok. Well...see you later. I hope." I stood up and dusted myself off, feeling my pants pocket to make sure my car keys were still there. Then I reached for the door, mentally planning how I'd smash a window with the bat and break free.

"You're a sucky friend." Cokie scowled as I was about to walk out.

I stopped in my tracks. "What?"

"It's true, you suck."

"Don't say that."

"Why not? You're just as much of a bully as *they* are."

I couldn't believe what I was hearing. Cokie had said *they*.

All the mean kids, she meant. The ones that followed us around, taunting us, telling us our pants were too short, too "last year," too *whatever*. They were the ones that made our lives a living hell, haunting us day and night with their invisible measuring stick. They were well-groomed, designer-clad vultures, hungrily waiting for us to fail, so they could swoop in and pick the flesh from our bones, pick out our eyes, and leave us dead, our spirits broken. In a way, they were like zombies, eating away at everything we stood for. And she said I was just like them.

"I'm not *that* bad," I said in my own defense.

"Yes, you are," she said in a low voice.

I didn't know what to say. A hot lump burned in my throat.

"You've never loved anyone, have you?"

I could feel the anger in her question, and it nearly stopped my heart. "That's not true," I said. "Maybe I have."

I loved Mr. Harrison but I couldn't admit it out loud. I couldn't own up to the fact that I had a torrid, freaky, schoolgirl crush on my teacher. That I fantasized about marrying him someday after I came back from law school, and doing married-people things to his body. And that he would become a stay-at-home dad and write copious books on philosophy from the comfort of our middle-class home, while I went out there to save the world from sexism, cruelty to animals, and mystery meat. Not that I didn't trust Cokie, but if anyone at school found out about my crush, there'd be no end to the ridicule.

My life would be over. So I kept it all hush-hush, even from my best friend, even though she hardly spoke anymore. Until now.

"Have you ever loved someone so much that you would do something crazy to prove you mattered?" she asked. "Even if it meant risking your life?"

Cokie was right. If I truly loved Mr. Harrison, I would try to save him. And maybe after I—I mean *we*—rescued him, he would rush into my arms and hold me tight, telling me with a gleam in his eye that he always knew I was his star student, and that I'd save the world some day. Plus, taking action and saving your men is the feminist thing to do. The truth is, I had been an awful feminist tonight. And an awful friend. "You're right. I would try to save the one I loved," I admitted. I felt my cheeks burning red. I had never given Cokie enough credit, but she was the smarter one in this friendship.

She smiled weakly, as if exhausted. "So, you're with me? You'll help me find Connor?"

I took a deep breath, and tried to speak with some measure of conviction. "Yes," I said. "I'm with you."

She jumped up and hugged me hard. "Thank you…you will never regret this."

I hoped she was right, because the more I thought about it, the more I realized that braving a school full of monsters to find our crushes was crazy. And dangerous. Oh God, what had I gotten myself into?

"SO, WHAT NOW?" I asked. "If we're going to do this right, we need a plan. How are we going to protect ourselves? Do you even know how to use that gun? Just because you're awesome at video games doesn't automatically mean you know what you're doing."

"You're right. But I have a secret that I haven't told you... or anyone else..."

"Huh? What secret?"

"My dad's been...taking me to the gun range..." Cokie cringed, like she was afraid of what I'd say.

"What?! Why haven't you told me?"

"I haven't told you because...because I thought you'd freak out, and be all snobby about it, like I'm some kind of violent psycho for knowing how to use a gun."

"Wait, why's your dad been taking you to the range?"

"Because I want to be a cop someday…like him."

"Does your mom know?!"

"Geez, forget that! It's not the point. Right now, having a gun could come in handy. It might be the only way to stay alive," Cokie said.

"Okay, so, when you train with your dad, how good are you?"

"I hit the bull's-eye most of the time."

"What do you mean, most?"

"About 95 percent."

The hair on the back of my neck prickled as I imagined us running through the halls, monsters lunging after us with gory mouths. I felt sick as I envisioned bullets shattering their heads and painting the halls with blood. Even though they were mindless flesh-eaters, it didn't seem right.

"Is there any other way to do this?" I pleaded.

"Don't worry. I don't want this to be a shoot-out. We're *not* on a zombie-hunting mission; we're on a people-rescuing, zombie-*avoidance* mission. We shoot only as a last resort. To defend ourselves."

I nodded like a bobblehead on speed. Her idea sounded good, and I wanted to believe it, but I had no idea if it was possible.

"You'll need to defend yourself too, you know. You know why I handed you that bat, right?"

I had taken the bat as a gut reaction in the heat of the

moment, but I didn't know what I would do with it, except stand there looking dumb with it raised in the air like a giant exclamation point. I didn't know the first thing about *anything* self-defense, aside from using a well-timed, caustic verbal insult on occasion. And I didn't know anything about zombies. I shook my head to say no.

"If you're backed into a corner, and you're in trouble, you have to swing for the head. Bash it like a piñata. It's the only way to make sure they're really, really dead."

I imagined being forced to defend myself, and swinging at a zombie's head with my bat, brains clattering all over the floor in a rainbow of brightly-wrapped piñata candy. Then I shuddered, because I knew it wouldn't really happen that way. No, in real life, it would be way less pretty and way more splatterific—red and raw like the exploded guts of a cherry pie. *Ugh.* I didn't think I could do it.

Cokie seemed to read my mind. "Trust me, if your life is on the line, you won't even think about it. You'll just do it."

I had my doubts. I had spent my life practicing *ahimsa*, not eating animals and avoiding the dissection of poor, unsuspecting frogs in Biology class. And aside from the occasional bug I may have squashed underfoot in my path through life, I hated violence of any kind. Was there a way to get through the night unharmed, without harming? Or was I delusional enough to think that I could avoid seeing blood? I realized that tonight, I was just like every other teenage girl: maybe I *was* crazy enough to do anything for love. I shuddered. Who was I becoming? But maybe it didn't matter. If I saved Mr. Harrison, it would all be worth it.

"So, where do we start?" I asked.

"From here...we should sweep the school. Find any kids that are hiding. We should be able to see inside each room from the hall. We rescue anyone we find. But first, we should go straight to the front office and try to use the intercom."

"Huh? Why would we do that?"

"If anyone is stuck in the school, they could call us back and we could find out exactly where they are, and go right there. It could save us time."

I nodded. She was full of ideas. Good ones. It was time to let Cokie wear the pants. "What about Connor? Where do you think he is?"

"There was a rumor that the B-boys were going to have a dance-off. A secret one. The location would be revealed on prom night, but only the cool kids knew the code."

"That's definitely not us."

"I know. But I have a feeling it's the music room in the basement. It's sound-proof and far away from everything, the perfect place to hide and have a secret party."

"That makes a lot of sense. I guess it's not that secret after all. What else?"

"Stay behind me, keep your voice low, and remember: *piñata*."

Piñata, I said to myself, searing the word into my mind once and for all.

Cokie studied my face, as though she were trying to make sure I understood our plan. "I think we're good," she said. "Let's go."

WE BOTH GOT UP and stretched, shaking off the stiffness from sitting for so long. As we approached the bathroom door, I realized Cokie had stopped stuttering when she called me out as a bully. She had found her voice tonight, and was showing me her true colors, a confidence she'd hidden for so long. She was way braver than I had ever been in my whole life. I had been a supreme coward, always using her to do my dirty work, but now it was *my* turn to roll up my sleeves. I shook because I knew I'd be putting my life on the line. But it was time to go do what I promised I would.

Cokie cracked the door again to make sure no one was outside, even though this hallway was supposedly sealed off from zombies. Then she pushed it all the way open, stepped through and waved me forward. We stepped around Taylor's body, still sprawled out where we had left him, killed by the fire extinguisher of doom. And though he was already dead, I secretly envisioned his perfect karma: the voracious creeps somehow finding his body and eating it.

Cokie stopped at the bag Taylor had left in the hall and rifled through it, shuffling through boxes. "I need more ammo for this handgun. This is pretty much the one my dad trains me on...it only has seven rounds. I don't want to use that other rifle he brought. It's way too big and scary. I've never practiced with anything but a handgun...." She held up some ammo and shoved it in her pockets. "Got 'em." She signaled for me to follow.

As we walked toward the hall that led to the rest of the school, it seemed that the zombies nearby had moved on. I paused by the floor-to-ceiling windows that made up the outside wall of the back of the building. Our school was perched high on the hill, and I could see far out from here, down to the fields below, and to the dark outline of trees that edged the woods behind them. A full moon hung low in the sky, casting an eerie glow on everything beneath its indiscriminate gaze. But storm clouds brewed on the horizon, threatening to take over and drown the world in darkness as they mushroomed into the sky, getting bigger, darker, angrier, hinting at their raw power.

Then I spotted *them*: more of the Infected, students who had gone off to the woods or to the field house to party, but had turned and now roamed the grounds in search of human flesh. They wandered aimlessly, shuffling in the moonlight, haunting figures in tuxedoes and gowns. Some of the girls tripped over their skirts and struggled to get up, fumbling over and over in the muddy field. Even as zombies, ridiculous prom gowns were the downfall of teenage girls, crippling them at the knees.

I squinted, trying to recognize the kids from afar. Though they were now monsters, they had once been like us. They had worried about grades, pimples, bad breath and bullying. They had friends, families, and pets. They had pinned some of their hopes and dreams on this night, their dreams about love. I had been too blind to see their humanity when it mattered. Even those who downright annoyed me, like Lila. I never took the time to know them as people. As *friends*. Aside from Cokie, I had no one. And I'd never get the chance to go back.

Maybe all of this was *my* karma. I was doomed to suffer a self-fulfilling prophecy: tonight, the very people whose mass conformity I once feared would eat me alive might actually just do it. Maybe it was exactly what I deserved. But I prayed for a second chance. Dear Buddha, if you're listening, please, please, please give me a second chance.

10

BEFORE WE ENTERED the next hallway, Cokie examined her pistol, then pressed a button on the side, releasing a thin red beam of light as she stood ready to push open the door with her hip.

"What is that light?" I whispered.

"It's a laser sight. It'll help me see my target, if I need it."

"Oh, um, wow, I didn't know those things were real."

"Yup, they are. Now, stay behind me." She grunted as she gave the door a push. It wouldn't budge. "Yikes. Can you help me? The door is stuck."

I clenched my stomach as we both heaved our weight against the door. As it opened, a girl's half-eaten body dragged along the floor, leaving a trail of blood.

"Oh-my-God," I said, clapping hand over my mouth as I fought the urge to heave up the contents of my gut. I stared at the girl. It was Willow Mackenzie, a tall, thin, gentle soul from my art class, who smiled to me every day even though no one else did, one of the few kids that had ever shown me any kindness. The left side of her face was gone—the face she had spent hours making perfect for prom. Though I didn't care for prom, Willow's loss was a tragic waste. She deserved better than this. I wanted to scream, to cry, to be anywhere but here, but I couldn't move. I was paralyzed by the destruction of beauty and youth.

Cokie tugged at my arm. "I know it's really sad...but we have to keep going."

We stepped gingerly around Willow, careful not to disturb what was left of her or step in her blood, but just as we did so, the locker room door fifty feet ahead of us flung open, and four snarling monsters spilled into the hall and ran toward us.

I froze in place again and screamed—the kind of scream that curls your hair when it comes out of your own mouth.

"Stay back," Cokie ordered. She had said she'd only shoot as a last resort, but we were already off to a bad start. She took aim at the closest one, accidentally flashing the laser in his eyes before she could sight her target. He screeched as his hands flew up to his eyes, and he dropped to the floor without even being shot. Cokie quickly did the same to the rest of them, and before we knew it, they all were down and howling, rolling on the floor in sheer agony.

"What just happened?" I yelled, relieved that no blood had been shed.

"I think the laser blinds them, which means we don't have to shoot! We just have knock them down and get past them. Now just *run!*"

I did as I was told, and heard the *slap-slap* of my sneakers as I bolted, trying to keep up with Cokie as we ran past their writhing bodies. I heard the door squeak behind me again, and turned to see five more creeps entering the hall behind us. I ran faster, but even as I hustled, I couldn't run fast *enough*. These weren't the slow zombies you heard horror geeks debate about in school. I cursed myself for never caring about gym class, and noted wryly that it's hard to run when you're just this side of having had one too many vegan brownies.

We rounded the corner into the next hallway, practically skidding out of control, and were greeted by more monsters from the other direction. There had to be ten or fifteen of them at least, and probably more on the way somewhere else in the school.

"Crap!" Cokie hissed and came to a stop. She looked the way I felt, like my heart might shatter from beating a million times a minute. We were surrounded. Cokie turned and held her arms up to aim, flashing the laser beam in a circle around us, blinding them until they shrieked and dropped, clutching their eyes like the others had done.

We were free to go, but had to dash around the fallen, an obstacle course that happened to bite and scratch. I said a million prayers as I hopped around them, making it almost all the way, until I tripped on a zombie girl's gown as she thrashed on her back. As I hit the floor, the bat flung out of my hand and rolled away. I scrambled toward it on my hands and knees trying to get it, but the girl had somehow grasped my leg, desperate for a taste. She clamped her teeth down hard, trying to bite through my jeans. I screeched for help, but Cokie had run into more creeps ahead. I was on my own. I kicked hard with my free leg, feeling bad as I bashed the girl's face in because she was someone that I recognized, and wasn't half bad in her pre-zombie days. But I kept going, smashing with my foot until she let go, wailing like a banshee as her face caved in. I panted as I came free, my heart jack-hammering in my chest as I reached for my bat and darted off.

"Come on," Cokie shouted from down the hall. "They're coming back!"

I glanced behind me and saw that the monsters farthest behind—the ones from the locker room—had gotten up and started their chase anew.

We sprinted ahead even faster, but as we approached the next corner, chilling screams stopped us cold.

"Oh crap, what is that?" I hissed under my breath.

Cokie held her gun ready and scurried to the edge of the hall, peering around the corner. "Oh, geez," she muttered, and turned away.

"*What?*"

"*Some poor girls are being eaten.*"

Against my better judgment, I snuck a glance around the corner like Cokie did, but instantly regretted it, knowing the image would be burned into my retinas until the day I died. I nearly convulsed from the sight, but couldn't look away. A mob of maybe nine or ten flesh-eaters fed in a frenzy, face down on their hands and knees in the guts of two girls that I couldn't recognize, whose struggling and screaming gave way to whimpering, then nothing—the sole remaining sound was that of the creeps gorging, growling as they ripped the girls apart.

"We have to get past them," Cokie whispered. "The office is right behind them."

I was paralyzed by fear. I didn't know if I'd be able to run toward the mob, even if Cokie brought them down with her laser. I looked past them and realized that the office lights were on. Someone had been there, and we might even find the door unlocked. We were seconds away from a temporary safe zone, and real telephones. If they even worked. I'd have to dig deep inside for a scrap of bravery and make a run for it.

One of the monsters looked up, glistening entrails hanging from his red-rimmed mouth. He spotted me, spat out the meat, and lurched up like a possessed marionette. The rest of the monsters looked up from their kill and lunged after him. Cokie leaped ahead, beaming across their eyes until they tumbled and screamed unholy screams, the kind that came from the deepest pits of hell.

"Quick," Cokie said. "Go!"

We darted around them, trying not to fall as they struggled on the linoleum. We made it to the front office and tested the door, which relented on the first try. We rushed in, closed it behind us, and twisted the lock.

THOUGH WE MADE it inside, the office's glass walls meant the room wasn't exactly maximum security. If the creeps got up again, we'd be in deep trouble. We'd have to work fast. Cokie pulled one of the chairs from along the walls and jammed it under the doorknob, although I wasn't sure if it would help, given the circumstances. Meanwhile, I ran to the secretary's desk and picked up the phone. I pressed it to my ear, hoping for a dial tone, but my heart sank when I realized the horrible truth: Taylor had cut the outside lines, leaving us stranded in a veritable meat grinder.

"It's dead," I said.

Cokie shook her head, knowing what Taylor had done without my saying another word.

She pushed another chair to the counter and stepped on the seat, struggling to reach the TV that hung from the ceiling. As it came to life, static flickered onscreen like driving snow. She scanned for a news channel. When a clear picture came into view, she climbed down, and we watched, silent and grim.

News cameras shook as they took in graphic scenes—people in suits with wild eyes lunging at each other with bloody faces, scratching and biting like ferocious animals. Police in fearsome black riot gear held them at bay with their shields, pushing them back into a swarming mass. A cold heaviness seeped from my heart, turning my arms and legs to lead, rendering me motionless. Neither of us spoke.

"Chaos in Seattle and beyond tonight," a newscaster announced from a panicked newsroom as footage rolled in the background. "People on the street are calling it *'zombieism'* for lack of a better word, though the exact nature or source of the illness is uncertain. It appears the disease began in schools, nursing homes and government buildings, and since then the infection has manifested in children, government workers, and the elderly. The CDC has called for an immediate quarantine, and several states across the U.S., including Washington, have called a state of emergency. So far, several law enforcement professionals have been injured or killed trying to contain the atrocity, and the National Guard has been called in to control the outbreak. All public buildings with a known quantity of the infected will be cleansed. All airports, major roads, and highways have been shut down to prevent the disease from spreading. Please keep your family indoors to avoid contamination. If a member of your family shows preliminary signs of infection—fever, sweating, lethargy, listlessness, and a sudden inability to form complete words or sentences—please isolate them quickly, as they may become violent. Also, please avoid all contact with potentially infectious bodily fluids."

We were glued to the screen, ignoring everything around us. More horrific footage rolled: foreboding black military helicopters pulsing in the sky like giant insects, torching a building with a firebomb. I shivered as I realized the building looked like a high school, though I didn't know where. It erupted into a ball of flames, and thick smoke rose into the night sky like an undulating, poisonous snake. But there was no more info, no more details. Just a very real threat of death by hellfire. Is this what they meant by cleansed? I forced myself to breathe and stay calm.

"Listen," I said. "I swear it looks like they're torching schools. I think that's what they meant by *cleansed*. They might torch *our* school."

Cokie stopped me and pointed to the TV, her eyes wide.

An image of Cokie's dad flashed on the screen. "Some of tonight's dead include local heroes," the reporter continued. "Joe Morimoto, a local police officer, died trying to contain the outbreak at the Federal building in downtown Seattle." Cokie wailed and fell to her knees at the news, and a sick feeling washed over me. Her dad had most likely been eaten alive, and if we survived tonight, her life would never be the same. I felt bad for her mom, too. Then my chest squeezed at the thought of my own parents. Were they safe? Would *my* life ever be the same?

As Cokie sobbed, I climbed up on the counter to shut off the television; I couldn't bear it anymore. I tried to comfort her, kneeling down and holding her while she convulsed with grief.

"My d-dad is g-gone...he's GONE...he was...the only person...who understood me. He was the one person...who didn't think it was weird that I played video games and...he was like a samurai...and...and I thought he might come save us...after we saved Connor. I wanted him...to be proud of me...I wanted him to be proud. I wanted to be a cop...like my dad."

"You can still be a cop," I whispered. "You can still be brave like your dad. You can keep his memory alive. This isn't the end. I promise you."

She nodded through her sobs and I couldn't think of anything else to say.

Soon she stopped and pulled away, her face puffy and swollen. She got up and reached for a tissue on the desk, and blew her nose.

"I'm sorry," she said.

"Don't be."

She nodded again.

"I meant what I said earlier," I warned, trying to be sensitive given what just happened to Cokie's dad. "I think they're torching schools. They—the government. We need to finish what we're doing, fast. We may not have much time."

"They...they have lots of buildings to torch, maybe...maybe we'll be one of the last since we're not in the city."

"We don't know that. If we want to find Connor, and anyone else, we'll have to hurry. Plus, look out into the hall."

We both scanned the space outside the front office. The creeps had started to get up, bumbling as their sight began to come back, and were joined by more from elsewhere in the school. They could see us through the window from the down the hall, and started to make their way toward us. It was only a matter of time before we were fair game.

Cokie blew her nose again quickly and threw the soggy, crumpled tissue in the trash by the desk. Then she reached for the intercom, pulled the microphone to her face and pressed the glowing red button.

She cleared her throat. "Hello...this is...Cokie Morimoto and Clarissa Hargrove," she said. "If anyone is hiding in the school, please stay where you are...it's not safe to escape on your own, but we'll find you and get you out. If anyone's here, please call us on the intercom and tell us where you are...thank you."

Feedback screeched over the PA system as she dropped the microphone in its cradle. I clapped my hands over my ears to block out the noise. A moment later, the red light flashed and the intercom rang.

Cokie's hand flew to pick up the receiver. "Hello?"

I pressed the speaker button so we could both hear, then shivered as an urgent male voice came through in fractured fits and starts. I couldn't even begin to make out what it said.

"Hello? *Hello?* Can you speak up? We can't hear you," Cokie said.

The voice started again, this time sounding even more urgent, but still garbled.

Cokie and I looked each other. "What if it's Connor?" she said.

What if it's Mr. Harrison? I thought. "We had better go."

"I can't hear you," Cokie said to the intercom. "But stay put. We'll find you, I promise."

We studied the intercom. The button that had lit up was labeled *Zone 2: cafeteria wing*. We knew exactly where we needed to go.

12

COKIE PUT DOWN the microphone and we surveyed the foyer again. A bigger mob was waiting for us, there had to have been about fifty of them. My breath began to falter. They moved closer to the office, pressing against the glass walls and snarling with malicious intent. The more they waited, the angrier they became, pounding their fists and smacking their palms on the window. With each sound my heart threatened to explode.

"Cokie, what if they break the glass?"

"Don't worry, I won't let them. Move the chair away from the door and get ready. We'll take off as soon as I'm done."

I stepped away from behind the desk to follow her orders. I moved the chair and stood by as she reactivated her laser, which had shut off while we were watching the news. The beam came alive again and she flicked it across each monster's vision. They took turns howling as they fell away from the window, dropping on top of each other in a seething mass. When only four were left, the red beam flickered and died.

"Shit," Cokie spat.

My heart flailed as she fumbled with her gun.

The wall of glass shattered in a rainfall of glittering sharp edges. I screamed as the four creeps tumbled through. A zombie boy knocked me over and landed on top of me, tangling my legs in his. In his pre-zombie days he had been a bully, always telling me how ugly he thought I was, and now he was trying to eat me. We wrestled in the broken glass, and I gripped his shoulders to hold his angry biting face away from mine, his teeth gnashing, his sky-blue eyes wild with hunger. I felt myself starting to weaken when a series of gunshots deafened my ears—Cokie must have shot the other three. My startled attacker reeled back to look up. I flipped him onto his back with my legs and scrambled backward to get away. He rushed me again on his hands and knees, ferocious in his need to feed. Cokie stepped forward and aimed her pistol. Another shot rang out, piercing the boy's forehead right before my eyes. His body slumped over my legs, hot blood spurting from his skull and soaking my jeans. I scrambled backwards on my hands again, sickened by the violence of survival. A sharp pain seared through my left hand. I held it up to inspect it. A thin red line oozed from the thick of edge of my palm, and broken glass studded my skin. I was nauseated and enthralled by the color of my blood, the essential fluid that kept my flesh alive, flesh the creeps so desperately craved. My head swam. Even though I had seen blood all night, it was the sight of my own that pushed me over the edge. I started to swoon.

My mind flashed back to the day I stopped eating animals. Mom had been up late, watching a documentary about meat production, and I happened to come downstairs in my pajamas. I padded up to the leather easy chair where she had fallen asleep, slack-jawed in front of the television. I knelt beside her without making a sound, watching the glowing screen in the dark, my eyes wide as animals moaned and met their grisly end, to be ground up and boxed and fed to the masses—to small children who loved their kitties and puppies and would never, ever harm a living thing. I ran to the bathroom, flipped up the toilet seat and retched the evening's hamburger dinner, still teeming and rare in my stomach. I watched as reddish brown bits floated up in the water, and I dry heaved, hoping to get rid of it all, hoping to expel life's horrific truth: from the moment we're born, we are all killers. My dad found me clutching the toilet bowl for dear life, curled up on my side.

"Are you ok, kid?" he said.

I shook my head. *I was not ok. I would never be ok.*

Dad knelt down on one knee and gave me his hand, lifting

me up so I could stand again. He held me steady as I bent over the pastel sink, washing my hands and face, scrubbing them cleaner than they'd ever been. I splashed stinging cold water over my eyes to numb the pain of seeing. My life had been changed forever.

Dad never spoke of that moment again. He would cast me knowing glances in the kitchen, but those glances soon evolved into teasing. I never understood why. But now I get it: in his own offbeat way, Dad was preparing me for the inevitable. In this cold, harsh world, everyone eventually gets eaten.

"CLARISSA," Cokie called out as she knelt beside me, snapping me out of my flashback, trying to bolster my head.

I looked up at her. She was visibly shaken.

"We need to get you bandaged up, *now*."

She helped me to my feet and handed me the bat to tuck under my arm. We treaded carefully through the space where the glass had shattered, and attempted to wind our way through the mass of stunned flesh-eaters. They thrashed as we moved between them like a deadly game of hopscotch. I was woozy, and almost fell once or twice, but forced myself to hold it together and keep my eyes on the prize: the clear space further down the lobby. Once we made it there, we moved quickly down the next hall to the nurse's office, leaving the creeps behind. When we reached the nurse's, the light was on and the door was unlocked.

"Hello? Anyone there?" Cokie stepped in, gun ready.

A quiet moan came from the back of the room, where two cots lined the walls. Cokie moved with caution, and I followed, making sure to lock the door behind me. We found Miss Stone, the school nurse, lying on the furthest cot. Her eyelids fluttered and her pale skin glistened with sweat. Damp, dark tendrils of hair stuck to the sides of her face as her head rolled from side to side, feverish and listless. She moaned again, and I shivered as I stepped back on instinct.

"She looks like she's coming down with it…the same thing that everyone else has," I whispered.

"Go now—take care of your hand. I'll stay here and keep watch."

I ran to the cabinets as I realized the truth of what she just said—that the nurse could wake up this second and decide we were food. And that Cokie would have to defend us while I took care of myself. I pushed the thought out of my mind and hustled to the cabinets, rifling through boxes and looking for antiseptic and bandages. Once I found them, I turned on the faucet and picked shards of glass from my skin, icy water running over my palm and swirling pink in the drain. When my hand was clean, I wiped the wound with the antiseptic, wincing as it stung. I pressed sterile gauze over the cut, and wrapped the bandage around it over and over, until my hand was protected.

A shriek rang out behind me, followed by a deafening gunshot that exploded in my eardrums. The sound shook me to my core. It was something I'd never get used to.

I turned around slowly with my heart in my teeth, afraid of what I would find. Cokie stood trembling by Miss Stone's limp, sprawled-out body, a red weeping hole in her forehead and a dark pool of blood spreading below.

Cokie looked up, panic-stricken and breathing fast. "I didn't want to, but...she attacked me...." She looked away, wiping her face on her sleeve. "I need to get the laser working again, because I really don't want to shoot anymore...it's way scarier than I thought it would be."

I nodded my head in agreement, adrenaline still coursing through my body from being startled.

She breathed deeply, shaking as she emptied the magazine out of the handle of her gun and laid it on the counter. "Gotta remember how to fix this," she said, voice quivering. "My dad taught me once..." She checked the top chamber for bullets, then pressed switches until the gun slid apart. I watched in awe as her fingers worked fast, like intelligent mechanical spiders, despite the stress of everything that just happened.

"I think...I think this laser has an auto shut-off after five minutes," she said. "But I had just turned it on again when it went out. So...either a screw is loose or the battery died. And if the battery died, we're in deep, because we don't have any way to replace it."

She dug in her pocket for a Swiss Army knife, opened it and flicked out a tiny screwdriver, the kind you use to fix glasses, or gun lasers, if that's what you're into. Cokie tweaked the screw, her face scrunched in concentration.

"There...that should do it. I hope."

I held my breath as she reassembled the gun, working as fast as before, and popped the magazine back in. She pressed a button on the side and the beam came alive again.

"Oh, thank heavens!" I blurted.

"Tell me about it."

I jumped, startled by the sound of bodies slamming on the door. Some of the creeps that had fallen outside had gotten up again and traced us to the nurse's office. Maybe they smelled the trail of blood that dripped from my hand. The scent had made me a beacon, one to an all-night diner serving the finest human flesh.

"Oh God, not again," I whispered.

"Shhh." Cokie shut off her laser beam again.

"What are you doing?" I asked, keeping my voice as low as possible.

"There are too many of them right now," she whispered back. "There's no way I can knock them over from this tiny window, and clear enough of a path. The hallway is too narrow. We should wait it out a bit, until they move on, then sneak out as fast as we can. Let's barricade ourselves in, just in case."

I nodded, though I wondered if staying here and waiting it out to stay alive mattered, because weren't we in danger of being blown sky high? But I remembered that we were staying alive to save others, and hoped that our gamble would pay off. Maybe we'd avoid extermination by fire long enough to get out of this room, and give others a chance to do the same. But what if we survived and found them only long enough to get torched on our way out the door? It was making my head hurt, like thinking about whether or not the chicken came first or the egg, a question we pondered in Philosophy class when we learned about Aristotle and Plutarch. I shook my head, stopping my brain from thinking useless thoughts, and joined Cokie in quietly moving the nurse's desk against the door. Then we sat down, and began our wait.

Cokie leaned forward in her chair as she watched the door intently. Neither of us spoke, not wanting to draw more attention to ourselves. Plus, it felt weird to even think about making small talk when, at any moment, we could die. I could barely hear the sound of our own breathing over the sound of snarling outside, and my neck muscles tightened as I flinched at each and every noise. I picked up my bat again and held it loosely in my right hand, balancing it on its end and wondering when I'd have to use it. I'd come so far without having to swing, but who knew what lay ahead.

Soon, the creeps started drifting away, and it got progressively quieter, until we heard almost nothing. At least nothing close by.

Cokie looked at me, and whispered. "I think we might be able to move soon."

I nodded. Cokie stood up and crawled up on top of the desk against the door to peek out the window. "Coast is mostly clear," she said as she climbed down. "We could roll out, but we have to be super careful. Remember, we're on our way to the cafeteria, because that's where the signal came over the intercom."

I thought about Mr. Harrison, and thought it just *had* to be him that tried to patch in from the teacher's lounge. I felt bad for Cokie, but I didn't think she'd be finding her man so quickly. My stomach twisted in nervousness and excitement as well as fear. If we made it over to the lounge, what if we *did* find Harrison? My heart started to race as we moved the desk away from the door. Things were about to get real again. Very, very, real.

Cokie opened the door a crack to peek down the hall, then poked her head out for a longer view. "We can run now and make it without any problems."

Run now and make it without any problems, she said. Oh, God, I hoped so.

"Ready?" she whispered.

My head nodded *yes* but my mind was silently screaming *no.*

Cokie pressed on her laser again, in case, well, you know.

"On three," she said. "One…two…"

We both darted out. I ran helter-skelter after her, my bandaged hand throbbing every time my feet hit the floor, my other hand gripping my bat like a vise. My lungs burned from the effort of running, but by some miracle, we ran freely for about thirty-five paces, and made it to the cafeteria doors without so much as a hitch. We almost crashed into them as we stopped cold, wanting to look through the windows and assess the situation instead of running in blind.

A wave of dread washed over my body at what I saw: a horde of the monsters mobbed outside the teacher's lounge like a pack of starving hyenas—maybe thirty or forty of them, at least. I didn't know if I had a shred of courage to move on. But I was sure Mr. Harrison was holed up in there. Mr. Harrison, the man of my dreams, the sole person who really understood me. I made up my mind. I had to go in there. I just *had* to.

13

WE HUDDLED OUTSIDE the cafeteria, making a quick plan.

"Let me run inside first," Cokie said. "There's enough room for me to run behind them and lure them away from the lounge, then you make a run for it and try to get in while I do my thing."

I swallowed hard. Cokie was risking her life for this one, and I would really owe her. I nodded, and she pushed open the door. The zombies' heads swiveled immediately, and all eyes were on us—every last soul-less one. Cokie sprinted past them, leading them to the farthest end of the cafeteria. They scrambled after her and away from the lounge, leaving me room to get there. I ran toward it and rattled the door-handle as I looked in the window. My heart pounded when I saw Mr. Harrison safe and sound, but with another teacher, Mrs. Blaine. They rushed over from the couch and unbarricaded the entrance, pushing away the table they shoved against it to let me in.

I made it safely inside, and the teachers shut the door behind me. A TV in the corner played nothing but static.

Mr. Harrison grabbed my shoulders. "Clarissa! I'm so glad to see you. Are you ok?"

I dropped my bat and nodded breathlessly, in part because I was terrified after what just happened, and in part because I was staring the love of my life in his sweet, low-carbon-footprint blue eyes.

"Where's Cokie?" Mr. Harrison continued in a barrage of questions. "We heard her over the intercom and couldn't believe what she said. Is she really trying to rescue people? And we saw on TV that her dad died trying to save people. Is she okay? Does she know?" Mr. Harrison asked.

"Tell us everything," Mrs. Blaine chimed in, taking my arm and guiding me to sit down. She was a young English teacher at my school, and it was rumored that half the boys had crushes on her, melting to puddles in her presence. Up close, I could see why: impossibly perky breasts, platinum starlet hair, flawless porcelain skin. She was totally hot—hotter than I'd be after a million makeovers, dye jobs, tummy tucks, and full-body waxes. Next to her, I was pretty much an ugly, knuckle-dragging Sasquatch baby. But I stopped caring. I was here now. With *him.*

And I would sure as hell rescue him if it was the last thing I did.

Mr. Harrison handed me a mug of water and they listened wide-eyed while I went back to the beginning, explaining how we wanted to stay and protest a little longer, but had come in to use the bathroom, then found Taylor about to mow everyone down, but we killed him by accident when we tried to stop him. And then the madness happened. I told them everything, and started to bawl like a toddler.

"Oh my gosh," Mrs. Blaine touched my arm, her face concerned. "We're scared too, but..." she struggled for words, "but... it's going to be okay. We'll find a way to get out of here just fine, together."

Mr. Harrison leaned in closer on my other side, putting his arm around me and rubbing my back. I had never been this close to him before, and I cried even harder, losing my mind over his touch.

Cokie darted into the room, and slammed the door behind her. "Is everyone all right?"

Mr. Harrison jumped up. "Oh my gosh—we're so glad to see you. We're fine. Clarissa was just telling us everything that's happened tonight. And we heard about Taylor. And your dad. We are so sorry."

Cokie's face fell. "Am I going to jail because of Taylor? Oh my God...I'm going to jail!" she wailed, and started crying too.

"No, no, no. It's going to be fine, I'm sure of it. It was self-defense," Mr. Harrison said. "Plus, after tonight, Taylor is the least of everyone's worries."

Mrs. Blaine hugged Cokie and I stood up next to Mr. Harrison. I studied him closer. His tie was loose, and a red mark blazed on the side of his neck—a blotch loosely shaped like a kiss. I looked over at Mrs. Blaine. I realized the back of her hair was mussed as though she had been sleeping on it. Her lipstick was smudged, and her navy satin dress was buttoned hastily, buttons in the wrong holes. I looked down at the floor. A lone, torn condom wrapper glinted on the dirty linoleum floor, reflecting sickly fluorescent lights.

"OHMYGOD! Were you guys fucking earlier?" I blurted. "You were here this whole time when everything went down. That's why you weren't in the gym! Then you stayed here because you were too afraid to come out!"

The teachers didn't say anything, didn't even chastise me for dropping the F-bomb in their faces—faces that wore expressions of guilt. Guilty as hell. Scarlet Letter red.

I started to cry again, and Mrs. Blaine shook her head.

Mr. Harrison pulled me off to the side, boring his eyes into mine, going into *Concerned Teacher* mode. "What's the matter?"

I wasn't going to say it. I had suffered enough humiliation. The one person I wanted to be with at the end of the world turned out to be an adulterous jerk-wad, screwing a married woman in the teacher's lounge when both of them should have been taking care of students and trying to save them. Vomit tickled the back of my throat. So far, trying to help my friend and save my fave teacher by putting my life in danger had been a total waste.

"Oh God...wait...I think I know what the matter is." He looked down at his feet, then back at me again, shaking his head, pained chagrin on his face.

Don't say it, I screamed inside my head. *Please don't say you know I have a crush on you!*

"Yeah, I think I know why you're upset..."

Great. You're not a total idiot, but I'd rather just forget this whole thing happened.

"If it makes you feel any better, I'm sorry."

It didn't, but I nodded my head anyway. Anything to get this over with.

He leaned in closer, lowering his voice. "You're my star student, so we've worked closely together on projects, and I pay lots of attention to you, so you think, well...that we have a 'thing,'" he said, making air quotes with his fingers. "Except, we don't. It was never my intent. It was a complete misunderstanding. Trust me, I think you're an amazing young woman, one of conviction, but I never ever meant to send you signals. But don't feel bad...this kind of thing happens all the time. Seriously, if I had a dime for every schoolgirl that's had a crush on me..."

I rolled my eyes. *Give me a break.*

"Well, like I said, I'm really sorry. I'm sure there's a guy your age who would love to be your boyfriend."

I tried not to gag, and was thankful when Cokie called over. "Guys, we really need to hurry. The zombies will get up any minute now and it will be harder to make a run for it."

I dried my tears on the sleeve of my sweater and pulled myself together. I had been a dope of astounding proportions and needed to put this behind me, fast.

"So, this is what we're going to do. You guys get behind us," Cokie said to the teachers. "Clarissa and I will run you to the closest exit and let you out to your cars, then we're going back in for more kids."

"What? No way. It's not safe. We should all stay here until we're rescued. We're safer behind closed doors," Mr. Harrison urged.

"No one is coming," I said. "At least, not for rescues."

"How do you know?"

"The news showed a school building being torched by a helicopter."

"You don't know that for a fact."

"They said, *'All buildings with a known quantity of the infected will be cleansed.'* Then they showed a school being torched, even though they didn't come out and say it was a school, directly."

"Look, I know you hate me right now, Clarissa, but the four of us should stay together," Mrs. Blaine said. "It's dangerous for you girls to go back out there, regardless of what we think is happening. Plus, you don't even know if anyone is left to rescue."

"My dad would *never* leave anyone behind, and neither will I," Cokie said, her small body shaking with the force of her belief. "We're going back, and we're rescuing more kids. We'll find whoever is left."

Mr. Harrison sighed. The teachers looked at each other, relaying silent thoughts of complete exasperation back and forth until Mrs. Blaine sighed and shrugged.

"Fine," Mr. Harrison said, rubbing his temples like we were hurting his brain. "If you're hell-bent on your rescue mission, we can't stop you. Just do what you think is right." He dropped the condescension and added, almost as if he cared, "And please be safe." He paused again. "Hey, Esther," he called Cokie by her real name, "one last thing…you stopped stuttering! What happened?"

I was about to tell them that she had found her voice tonight, that she was the bravest kid that ever lived, and no one would ever bully her again, but we were startled by noise outside. The creeps were on the hunt again, and began to rattle our cage.

Cokie shook her head. "We waited too long. I need to figure out our next move." She hustled toward the door, standing beside it with gun ready, her chest rising and falling as she took deep breaths, thinking and biding her time.

Meanwhile, something was off. The teachers had grown paler and paler as we were speaking. Their skin had begun to glisten with sweat, and dark patches had formed under their eyes.

"Oh my gosh, I don't feel so good..." Mrs. Blaine murmured, fumbling for the leather couch.

"Ugh...me either. I feel...terrible..." Mr. Harrison muttered, doing the same.

This couldn't be happening. They were getting sick right before our eyes. We had maybe a minute left before they tried to eat us. I watched them flop onto the couch, soaking their clothes with sweat, their heads rolling listlessly to the side as their eyelids flickered open and closed.

"Cokieeeeee..." I said, looking around me. My bat was on the other side of the room, leaning against the wall, asleep on the job. In other words, totally useless.

The teachers rocketed from the couch with a growl. A scream ripped my throat as I flipped up a lunch table, putting a barrier between us. They stumbled backward, scrambling to get up again.

Cokie aimed her gun at the teachers, hands shaking. *"Shit!"* Her laser was dead again.

14

OUR ZOMBIFIED TEACHERS regained their footing, scrambling around to get past the table. I flipped up another one to hold them back, and another, and another.

"There's no way I can fix this laser fast enough!" Cokie wailed, hands and gun still pointed, and shaking.

"Should we run?"

"We'll be too mobbed out there—it's either shoot here or out there...*shit!*"

"Do what you have to do!" I clapped my hands to my ears and got down low, closing my eyes so I wouldn't see the splatter.

Two shots numbed my hearing. I opened my eyes and looked up. The monsters had been slain, their bodies splayed like rag dolls across tables and chairs. I looked at Cokie. She went limp, falling backward against the wall as she slid to the floor. I ran over and knelt beside her. She stared ahead into space and didn't speak.

"Are you ok?" I whispered, ignoring the noise outside, the creeps clamoring to get in.

She trembled without making a sound, and kept staring.

"You did what you needed to save us. They weren't people any more—they were monsters. Anyone can see that. Talk to me. Please."

Still nothing.

"Do you want to go home?" I asked gently. "We don't have to stay. We should just try to make it out alive. I don't think we can handle what we're trying to do. I just don't."

My question had broken through. She turned sharply to face me, her lip quivering. "No...we can't leave! If my dad were here, he would never go without saving as many people as he could. We still need to try to find Connor...and anyone else!" Her eyes pleaded.

I needed a moment to think about what we were doing, and what to say next. I paused, biting my lip as my gut wrenched with heartache for my best friend. I knew that saying the wrong thing could crush her. She didn't have her dad anymore, all she had left was what he taught her. The only thing that kept Cokie going was living for others, not for herself. Even if it meant the utmost danger.

I took a deep breath, and spoke. "Do you remember when Mr. Harrison was asking when you stopped stuttering?"

"Yeah." She wiped a stray tear with a finger.

"I was going to tell him that you were the bravest girl on the planet and you could fight anything and do anything you set your mind to. That no one else is as bad-ass as you are."

"Really?" she sniffled. "You...you were going to say that?"

"Yup."

"You really, really meant it?"

"I still do."

She nodded. I felt my heart expand three sizes as we both fell quiet.

Cokie dried her eyes on the grimy sleeve of her hoodie. "Thank you for being my friend." She paused. "Why are you my friend again? I mean, forget all the stuff you just said. No one else is my friend." She shook her head, fighting back more sniffles.

"I don't know...why are you *my* friend? I mean, I'm no prize. All the other kids seem to think I'm bat-shit crazy. Possibly because I am."

"Because...because we've known each other since first grade. And you're the only one who talks to me. You've never made fun of my stutter."

"Well, you're the only one who talks to *me*," I said.

It was true. We had been each other's friends for as long as

I can remember, but were each other's friends because no one else wanted us. We were the Freaks. The Misfits. We looked different and thought different and dressed different. Maybe that made us special...but then why did being special hurt so much? Why was being different so lonely?

I needed to cheer Cokie up. I thought about Mr. Harrison, and how ridiculous it was that I had a crush on him. "Did you know I had a crush on Mr. Harrison?" I said.

"Yup," Cokie smiled through her tears.

"How? I tried so hard not to show it."

"Because, um...you act like a weirdo every time he walks by."

"Ugh. I thought I was being subtle this whole time. "

Cokie shook her head. "Nope...not very subtle at all."

"I'm such a dork. He turned out to be a jerk. Why am I so dumb that I have to have a crush on teacher? It's really weird and crazy, right? I mean, why couldn't I love a real boy? What kind of girl falls in love with a teacher? It's totally sick! Pervy, even! Oh, God!"

"Well, Mr. Harrison was kinda hot."

"Yeah, he was..."

"And he recycled."

"Yeah. And he had that electric car, and he rescued animals. He was kind of perfect. A perfect...dirtbag." I sighed. "I'm an idiot, though. Really, what did I expect?"

Cokie gave a half-hearted shrug. The point was obviously

moot, and not worth discussing anymore.

I thought about what I wasn't brave enough to say to Cokie, or to anyone. The truth was, Mr. Harrison was one of the few people who didn't treat me like I was crazy. Who listened when I spoke. Who believed that standing up for things mattered more than the clothes you wore, or the car you drove. Even if he was kind of a player.

I thought about real boys. I thought about them in all their pimply, sweaty, awkward glory. And the ones that weren't pimply or sweaty seemed to be made out of orange plastic, the kind that Ken dolls were made of. Surely there was more to the male teenage species? I was embarrassed at myself. If I was a feminist, then I didn't really need boys. Or did I? Maybe there was something in my body that was making me a little crazy. *Boy* crazy. Was this natural? Maybe it was. Maybe there was a boy out there for *me?* Was this even possible?

"Well," Cokie said, as if she read my mind. "There are some real boys that seem to like you. Or at least seem nice."

"Yeah?" I said, completely unsold. "Who?"

"There's…that stoner kid who steals brownies from your table every day…"

I shook my head and groaned. "Cokes, no way. Underachiever city. He's smart, but doesn't even try in school. He's never going to amount to anything."

"But he's *nice*," she insisted.

"And smells funny. Why do stoners think we can't smell their fumes?"

"Okay, okay…forget him."

"See? Real boys aren't happening for me."

"Don't say that."

I sighed.

"Just keep an open mind. You don't know who's out there. Maybe…maybe there's someone you haven't given a chance yet."

Cokie was right, but I realized this whole conversation was actually kind of useless. "Let's forget about teen romance for yours truly, for now. Seriously, we should just concentrate on finding Connor." I paused for a beat. "You never told me why you like him."

"Well, duh…he's really cute."

"Ok, right, I'm a dope. He's totally cute. But really, why?"

Cokie took a deep breath and began to gush. "I play video games online with him and a whole bunch of other kids, and he doesn't know that it's me, and that I'm a girl. But he's the only one that doesn't talk smack about the other girls that play. The other boys are really mean…they say that girls ruin the game…that we're all just bitches and we like to brag that we're girls and we're awesome. But I never do. And Connor never says anything like that. And in art class, he's even kind of nice to me. He's one of the few kids who doesn't make fun of me when I stutter. So, I've been really crushing on him…and hoped he would go to prom with me. Except…you know." She looked down at her feet.

"I know. I am so sorry. It's all my fault."

"Don't be sorry…we already talked about this. It's good that I wasn't in there…with *them*."

"I know."

We both took a deep breath. The creeps on the other side of the door were freaking me out, but we needed to keep moving if we wanted to get out of here. "So, are you feeling better?" I asked. "We should get going."

"Wait…I need to fix my laser sight again. The screw keeps coming loose."

"Totally. Go for it." Anything to forestall the need to kill.

She picked it apart again right before my eyes, tweaked a screw, and reassembled it methodically. She pressed the laser button again, and the beam shot across the room. I let out a long, slow sigh. We'd make it out to our next destination without a bloodbath. At least, I *hoped* we would. All we needed was our next plan. "So, what now?" I asked.

"Connor. Secret room. Dance-off."

I imagined that the dance-off had long been finished, and that we'd be lucky if we found anyone alive…or intact. I shuddered as I imagined the worst…a breakdance party turned to a flesh-eating orgy, boys and girls on their hands and knees like a pack of wild dogs, deep in the guts of their friends. My heart began to thrash. I shook my head, trying to wipe the thought from my mind. If I was going to make it, I needed to pretend like everything would be fine. *Everything will be fine*, I told myself, sweating as the lounge doors banged louder and louder under the weight of the monsters. *Everything. Will. Be. Fine.*

"Ready to go?" Cokie asked, standing up and shaking herself off.

I stood up beside her, retrieved my bat, and did the same, pushing a wellspring of fear back down, deep into my body where I hoped it would never burst free. "I'm ready...ready as I'll ever be."

15

THE MONSTERS BECAME even more agitated as we approached the door. They snarled louder with hunger and excitement, each sound causing me to jump. I took deep breaths to quell my anxiety. We were like chum in the water, the tiniest smell of our flesh causing a feeding frenzy. If we weren't careful, we'd be ripped to bits. *Don't think about it,* I told myself. *Just. Don't. Think!*

Cokie took in the scene through the narrow window, not flinching from the faces that pressed against it, distorted expressions like gargoyle masks, lips marred with blood. "Crap. They're blocking us in."

"Can you still laser them?" I asked.

She shook her head. "I don't know if I can. There are too

many, and this window is pretty small. I might not be able to get them all."

"Just try it," I begged.

She nodded, taking another deep breath before backing up a few feet to aim the beam through the slim field of vision, her brow furrowed as she held the gun steady. She dropped the ones closest to the door, every shriek making me wince as they fell away. Then a few more scrambled forward to take their place, leering at us through the window, and she did it again, repeating the process until she had gotten them all, bit by bit.

"Ok, we have to go, *now,*" she said, getting ready to push open the door.

I moved closer, preparing myself to hustle, but snuck a last glance at Mr. Harrison, at the empty shell of a person who had to be put down like a rabid mongrel. I averted my eyes quickly, hoping to forget him forever.

"And watch yourself," Cokie whispered before we set out across the biter gauntlet.

I nodded *yes* really hard. *Yes, yes, yes.*

Cokie twisted the knob, and we thrust our bodies against the door, heaving against the creeps that blocked our way. They screeched at their helplessness, flailing blindly on the floor.

My pulse throbbed as we hurried between them, trying to anticipate when they'd kick or swipe. A boy's leg shot out sideways, knocking Cokie off balance. She howled and fell, and the gun flew from her hand, clattering and spinning across the linoleum. I screamed as two zombie girls in pink satin clung blindly to Cokie's legs, trying to bite through her skater pants while holding tight with tanned arms.

I lunged toward them, my heart wanting to explode from my chest. I swung my bat low like a murderous golf club, aiming for one zombie girl's up-do, then another, praying I wouldn't hit Cokie. Their skulls cracked audibly and their arms went slack as dark puddles oozed beneath them with sickening speed. Cokie struggled to stand. I gave her my hand, helping her up to run and get her gun. She dashed to the corner where it had landed, and scooped it up, looking grateful. I ran after her and stood there panting, watching the puddle spread from a safe distance while nausea rose in my body, about to take over my senses.

"Oh no, I think I'm going to be sick," I said. I bent over, placing my hands on my thighs, feeling the world spin, trying to take deep, cleansing breaths like I'd learned in yoga class.

"No," Cokie said. "*No-no-no-no.* Don't get sick. Not here, not now. We need to run." She grabbed my sleeve, yanking me away from the twitching munchers who would regain their sight any minute now.

16

I FORCED MYSELF to swallow my nausea, and we peeked through the lunchroom doors to see if the coast was clear. Three or four monsters wandered down the ends of each hall, both the one straight ahead of us that led to the basement stairs, and the one to the right that led back to where we came from, the front of the school. I squinted to get a closer look. Some of the creeps appeared to be mangled, as though their skin disintegrated more the longer they were sick. Chunks of their flesh peeled back, revealing blood and bone. One dragged a bloody stump of a leg that peeked out from under her gown, foot missing at the ankle, painting the floor red as she went. Another was missing both hands. But not all were like this. I shuddered. *What was going on?*

Cokie looked from side to side. "Only a couple here and there," she said. "Looks like some are slowing down, getting sicker. This could be good. Let's go." She readied her pistol and laser and we snuck out, heading toward the basement stairwell that led to the music room where Connor might be. The creeps at the far end turned to face us and lurched toward us in a shuffle-run, StumpGirl dragging her leg behind her. Cokie held them at bay with a few simple flicks of the wrist, flashing the beam in their eyes. They howled and fell like the others had done, and we were free to move down the stairs.

Cokie entered the stairwell first, keeping her gun ready as she began a slow descent, laser slicing the air on our way down. I was worried about an ambush, and held my bat ready, hearing the clang of metal stairs below my feet. The fluorescent light above flickered and buzzed like it was too weak to go on, and could leave us in the dark at any moment.

Our feet touched the bottom step, and the hall before us was dim and cold, colder than anywhere else in the school, like a meat locker. Goosebumps dotted my arms as we moved along. Another bulb blinked, making me wonder how much time we had before things went horribly wrong. Suddenly, Cokie stopped in her tracks.

"Shh...do you hear it?"

"Hear what?"

"The thumping."

I strained to listen. I *did* hear it. *"Yes,"* I whispered.

"Sounds like hip-hop…coming from around the corner," Cokie said, her face growing more serious by the second.

We had reached our destination, our moment of truth. The culmination of Cokie's whole night was here and now: Connor, her entire reason for staying, might be alive or dead…or worse. I prayed for my best friend's sake that he was fine. Maybe he'd be just a little bruised and scared, but we could save him.

Cokie waved me to come with her and we scooted around the bend toward the music room, far down the hall like the seventh circle of hell, where kids who played jazz flute were banished until the end of time. The thumping grew louder with each step, and even from this far I saw strobe lights flashing through the window, illuminating the dark room in spastic fits. My spine tingled. Whatever was going on in there, it was sure to be the party of the century.

17

WE MOVED CLOSER to the music room, about fifty paces from
where we rounded the bend. The sound pulsed louder, and
giant, Mothra-sized butterflies multiplied in my stomach, fighting
their way upward. I swallowed them back down, and clutched
my bat so hard I'm sure my knuckles turned white.

When we got to the door, I sucked in my breath, realizing
that in a matter of seconds everything would be different, that
Cokie's hope might be shattered. Muffled hip-hop rattled the
walls. I looked at Cokie, her face glowing under the strobes that
flickered through the glass as she pressed in closer, trying to
spot Connor.

"Oh my God," she moaned.

I leaned in to look over her shoulder, reeling at what I saw. Girls and boys writhed in agony on blue floor mats as light blinded the room one second at a time. I couldn't tell who was who and what was what. "All the kids look sick," I said. "But I think the strobes are making them crazy."

"Connor's supposed to be in there. But…but I don't see him!" Her voice had an edge of desperation.

"What should we do?" I asked.

"I don't know…I think…I think I still want to go in there! Maybe he *is* in there, somewhere…maybe he's hiding! I just need to find out!" She continued to stare inside, like staring might make Connor appear faster, or keep him alive.

We had come all this way and hadn't rescued a single soul. Was it over? If he was sick, we'd be wasting our time and putting our lives in danger. "What if he's sick, Cokie? Why would we even go in there?"

"I don't know…I don't know!" Her breathing grew shallow, like she might hyperventilate.

I tugged at her sleeve. "Come on. We should leave. I'm not sure there's a point in staying anymore. Connor could be gone, and we could be sky-high in a mushroom cloud before we know it."

She ignored me, pressing her face against the window.

"It doesn't look good, Cokie. We can't see him, they all look sick, Maybe sicker than the other kids we've seen. This has officially turned into a suicide mission."

She turned to face me, her eyes flashing. "You promised you'd help, but even if you don't, I'm going in there whether you like it or not. All my life, I've done *everything* you've ever asked me to do, because I love you, because you are my friend and I would do *anything* for you, even if it's super embarrassing, because that's what friends do for each other, like wearing that *stupid* bunny suit, or skipping out on prom because it means something to you. But just this once, I want to do what *I* want to do. You know what, boss? I'm tired of being told what to do. *I'm tired of being your monkey!*"

I was stunned. Nobody had ever spoken to me that way before, but I totally deserved it. She had finally said the whole, unadulterated truth. Cokie was right, she'd always had my back, no matter how ridiculous the situation or the potential for social embarrassment. I owed her one last chance to be herself, to be the mistress of her own destiny, whatever it held. I nodded, choking back tears. "Okay, I'm sorry. You should do what you think is right. We've come this far. We might as well."

Cokie nodded, not wasting any more time. Her hands shook as she slowly reached for the doorknob, then gripped and twisted it, opening the door with care. A blast of music assaulted our eardrums, and strobes lit up Cokie's silhouette. She looked back at me over her shoulder. "I'm going in."

A chill fell over me as she stepped in tentatively, then walked in farther, laser piercing the throbbing darkness. I followed, swearing like I had Tourrette's as I squinted to see, both of us scanning the room frantically. The creeps twitched violently on the mats, foaming at the mouth—a freak show under blinding flickering lights. Their faces were contorted and pieces of their skin and body parts had fallen off, like the creeps we'd seen in the hall upstairs. Between the freaks lay half-eaten dead kids in torn tuxes and gowns. Oozing holes gaped where chunks of flesh had been ripped out, exposing arm and leg bones. Faces were half-gone, skin peeled back to reveal teeth and jaws. Eyes were scooped out of their sockets. Intestines trailed on the mats. Then I recognized Asha, poor sweet Asha from before, only dead and mangled. I was paralyzed. It was too horrible to see, yet I stood shaking at the edge of the mat, unable to look away. This is what my high school life had become—a horror show of epic, mind-fuck proportions. *What is seen can't be unseen*, my dad had said the day I became vegan. I'd never be the same again.

"I don't see Connor," Cokie hissed over the music. "This *sucks!"*

I willed myself to turn away, and forced myself to think. "We need to go," I yelled. "If he's not here, we should move on."

"WAIT!" A voice called out in the darkness, fighting to be heard over the music. "Cokie? Is that you?"

We looked up toward the back of the room. We could make out the shape of a skinny kid in a white tux, laying flat on top of the wall of storage cabinets, his head just inches from the ceiling tiles. *Connor?*

"Oh my God!" Cokie shouted to the boy. "Are you okay?"

"Yeah!" he shouted back. "I'm just too scared to come down!"

"Just stay there. We'll help you!"

Out of nowhere, the thumping hip-hop came to a stop. So did the strobes. Had the school lost power? *Craptastic.*

"Oh, no. I was counting on the strobes to keep them down," Cokie called out in the dark. "And I can't see. Clarissa, does your phone have a flashlight?"

I searched in my pocket for my cell phone, my bandaged hand making it difficult. I pressed the flashlight button and a weak light pooled in the room. The monsters moaned on the floor, rolling their heads from side to side, trying to shake off the strobe-sickness. Cokie stepped around them, maneuvering closer to Connor. She placed a chair next to the cabinet and stood on it, offering him a hand. He swung his legs out fast and Cokie helped him slide onto the chair.

"How did you get up here without a chair?" she asked. "It's really high."

"Parkour classes. And fear. When you're *really* scared, you'll scurry up anything to get away."

"Right," Cokie said, clearing her throat. Then she hopped down from the chair, taking his hand and helping him down too.

"Come on, guys. *Hurry,*" I urged.

Cokie and Connor hustled around the mat, careful to avoid

being grabbed or kicked. It looked like the strobe-sickness was wearing off. They flailed less, becoming calmer. I heard a growl and looked back. A zombie girl in a midnight-blue dress rolled to her side just as Cokie and Connor passed by, and her eyes flicked open. Zombie Girl's eyes met mine.

Panic seized my brain.

Shit.

She flipped over, scrambling on her hands and knees, growling as she aimed for my friends' ankles.

I screamed.

But I also ran at her and swung my bat with my free hand. It was awkward and I merely managed to stun her, so I swung again.

This time the bat *thwacked* loud against the side of her head, mashing her skull and sending a spray of blood and brains into the music room.

I couldn't believe what I was becoming. I was getting too comfortable with killing, it seemed—from the two zombie girls in the lunchroom only five minutes ago, to *this*—the point where I was a one-handed, cold-blooded, flashlight-holding zombie-killer in the name of friendship. But before I got lost in my own horror, Cokie pushed me toward the door.

18

WE ESCAPED the music room just as more creeps recovered and came to their feet with a growl. We slammed the door behind us, and the three of us stood in the hall, panting in the dark, with nothing but the flashlight on my cell phone to light the way. Then the overhead lights flashed on again, and I was relieved that the power was back. This hallway was safe—the only zombies on this floor were trapped in the music room—so we took a moment to collect our wits.

"Holy crap," Connor muttered. "That was crazy." He took another breath, looked at Cokie, and tapped her on the shoulder. "Thanks for coming to get me. I owe you a solid."

Cokie didn't look at him, but looked at her feet instead. "You're welcome."

"And you," he nodded at me, "I've always thought you were kinda weird, but I'd take weird any day after this. Nice shot, zombie huntress."

I am NOT a zombie huntress, I groaned in my head at the thought of my ugly, violent bat-swing. I decided to set the record straight. "Dude, you're welcome, but Cokie's the real hero. It was her idea to come get you, and you have no idea how many freaks she handled on the way down to get you."

"What? Me? Really?" He stared at her in disbelief.

"Well, everyone..." Cokie chimed in. "I came to get anyone I could find."

"Oh, yeah, cool," Connor said, relaxing his stance as he did the bro-nod, tipping his chin upward once in solidarity. "Totally bad-ass. For reals."

Cokie blushed.

"You didn't hear us over the intercom?" I asked.

"Nope, I guess the music was too loud," Connor said. "But I'm still glad you found me."

"We should go, you guys," Cokie said. "They could blow up the school, remember?"

"What?" Connor said.

"Yeah," Cokie said. "We'll explain later. We need to bolt."

"Ok," he said. "Then let's roll."

"Hold on," I said, stopping them both. There was something that had to be done. We had come this far for a reason. I wasn't about to let Cokie waste this opportunity to let Connor know how she really felt. This couldn't wait. Love is more important than the end of the world. "This is crazy, but, before we go, I have to say something."

They both turned to face me.

"Clarissa, not now, we really need to leave," Cokie said. She looked embarrassed, like she could read my mind and knew what I was about to say. I'd never had a reputation for keeping my mouth shut, and I wasn't about to start now.

"Just wait a sec. Connor, Cokie wanted to ask you to prom, but she couldn't because of me," I blurted. "She thinks you're great because you don't make fun of her and you don't talk smack about the girl gamers online."

Connor looked at me, stunned.

"Clarissa, geez, I said, *not now!*" Cokie spat under her breath. "Save it for later!"

"What do you mean?" Connor said. He turned to face Cokie. "You play online with me?"

She nodded. "I'm SamuraiXX97," she mumbled.

"What?! You're SamuraiXX97? I thought you were a dude. Dang girl, you've got mad skills."

I felt bad, because Cokie looked like she wanted to crawl into a hole and die. She wasn't good at this flirting stuff, and maybe I wasn't much better, but I wanted her to break the ice.

"Um, so what's SamuraiXX97 stand for?" Connor asked.

"You know in science class...when we learned about XX and XY chromosomes? Well, girls have XX chromosomes. It was kind of a secret code...to let you know I was a girl. A Japanese girl. And 97...that's my birthday."

"Uh, cool, cool," Connor said. He looked down at his feet, fidgeting.

I waited for something to happen. They stood there, looking awkward, like they were praying for meteorites to hit them both. I'd had enough. I was going to be blunt. I pulled Connor aside to have a "private" chat with him—as private as I could, given that Cokie was standing right there.

"Look," I leaned in close and said in a low voice, "this may be our last night on Earth, and Cokie was really hoping to get a dance with you. I mean, you said you owe her a solid, right? Maybe you could dance with her, right here and now...we did risk our lives to save you."

He barely looked me in the eye. Behind him, Cokie looked even more embarrassed. Worse, her face was red and she bit her lower lip, looking like she was holding back a flood of waterworks. Maybe I had made a mistake by saying what I'd said. Connor just stood there, frozen. It wasn't going the way I had planned. I'd hoped he'd ask her to a spur-of-the moment prom dance that very second, music or no music, zombies or no zombies, bombs or no bombs, but maybe that was insane. It was obvious now that it wasn't going to happen, at least not tonight. God, I was so bad at all this romance stuff. I should have just left well enough alone.

Connor cleared his throat, and turned toward Cokie, holding out his arms, silently asking her to dance.

Her eyes welled. "But we have no music," she whispered.

"We don't need music," he whispered back.

"But they might bomb the school."

"That's true, they could. Or we could die a gajillion other ways tonight. We might not even make it down the next hallway."

"But…"

"Please, just dance with me a little. It can be ten seconds, if that. If this is our last night on Earth, don't you want a prom dance? The prom dance of your dreams before you go *boom?*" He smiled impishly, the same Connor I remembered from the halls, a cutie who loved to please the ladies. Except now he was pleasing someone very special to me: my best friend, Cokie.

She stepped into his arms, and they danced awkwardly, despite the fact that Connor was supposedly a good dancer. I guess slow-dancing is harder than break-dancing, but that didn't matter. He was making my friend happy and that's all that counted. Nor did it matter that Cokie wasn't wearing a prom dress or sexy heels, or didn't have her hair in a perfect up-do. She was happy without all of that stuff. She rested her chin on his shoulder as they danced in a slow, clumsy circle to imaginary music. Her prom dream had come true. My heart swelled with hope. Maybe I had been a good friend, after all.

Connor pulled her in closer and started sniffing her hair and nuzzling her neck. Out of nowhere he had become horny-romantic, and it was completely over the top.

"Connor, what are you doing?" she asked, struggling to push back.

I panicked. Something wasn't right.

Suddenly Connor lunged, grabbing her head with vicious force and biting down on her face. A blood-curdling scream shot from her mouth and I snapped into action, smashing the backs of his knees. He lost his grip and Cokie slipped free, pulling her pistol out of her pocket. An ear-blasting shot rang out as she nailed him between the eyes. He dropped to the floor, bright red blood marring the white of his tux and pooling below him on the gray cement.

Cokie stood still, bleeding and wild-eyed, until her whole body gave way to trembling. She dropped her gun. "OhmyGod... Oh...my...God!" She began to whimper. "I-I... killed him... I had to...h-he bit me...*he bit me!* Clarissa, what am I going to do?"

"I don't know," I said, panicking. I felt ill, knowing the seriousness of what had just happened. It was my fault he had bitten her. I had insisted on the dance.

Me. My fault.

"You know that I'm going to turn, right?" Her eyes brimmed with desperation. "I'm going to become just like them."

"We don't know that," I lied. "We *don't know*."

"Yes we do, Clarissa. *Yes we do*. It only means one thing." Her lower lip trembled.

I knew what she was going to say, and I didn't want to hear it.

"It means you have to kill me," she said. *"You have to shoot me, Clarissa*. You have to." Tears streamed from her eyes.

I cried too as I gasped out my words. "I can't shoot you, Cokie. You know I can't do it. Please don't ask me to do it. Please. Because I won't. *I can't kill my best friend.*"

"You have to!" she roared through choking sobs. *"You have to!"*

"No. I can't do it. *I can't.*"

"Fuck you, Clarissa. It's the one thing I'm asking of you now, as a friend, and you won't do it. SO FUCK YOU. I'm taking matters into my own hands."

She crouched low to the ground and picked up her gun with shaking hands.

I wanted to wrestle it away from her, but knew that was just as dangerous. "No, don't do this," I said, trying to reason with her. "Don't do this. Please...please...please..."

My words had fallen on deaf ears. She lifted the gun to her head and opened her mouth.

I screamed at her to stop.

I closed my eyes, afraid of what I'd see. The blast was loud.

I slumped to the floor and howled at the top of my lungs, knowing that I had failed. My best friend had taken her own life. And I hadn't been able to stop it.

19

I WAS *mo ni fukushite*, in mourning.

I wailed beside Cokie's body for what seemed like an eternity, until my lungs ached and my eyes burned, and I couldn't cry another drop. I cradled her bloody head in my lap, not caring that I was covered in gore, and stroked her hair, brushing it aside from her pale, moon-shaped face. I saw her eyes up close for the first time in my life. They glinted like flashing steel, the color of a samurai's heart.

It's totally true what they say, that you don't truly appreciate someone until it's too late, until they're gone. I thought about all the things I wanted to tell Cokie. There were so many, but I had missed my chance. It happened so fast. There had been no goodbyes. Just angry last words, a shot, then silence.

Even though she was gone, I needed to do something to show her that I cared, that her last moments hadn't been in vain. I stood up and grunted as I pulled her by the hands, moving her body next to Connor's and placing them arm in arm. If they couldn't be each other's prom dates in life, at least they could be together in death. I took the sad, wilted flower from his lapel and pinned it on her sweatshirt, a prom night corsage for a girl who'd never had one.

"Happy Prom Night, dear girl," I whispered, and kissed her cheek. "I will always love you."

As I gently closed her eyelids, I realized I'd never felt so alone in my life.

I sat on the floor, overcome by emotion. I had no more reason to fight, no more reason to live. But I wasn't even sure I was brave enough to off myself.

I fantasized about sacrificing myself to the sheep I once scorned, the spray-tanned Meat Eaters that now roamed the hidden recesses of the school, consuming each other without care, the way they'd always done. Maybe those zombies were better off than I was. They had no existential thoughts. No feeling, no pain. Just pure, mindless bliss. Maybe I could join them and end my suffering once and for all. I thought about going upstairs and standing in the hallway, with my arms wide open in a gesture that said, *"Welcome, zombies. You win. Make me one of your own."* I imagined them overtaking me, clawing, biting, and scratching as they dragged me down and fed on my entrails. It would hurt like hell, but it would be over quickly. Then I could become one of them, and the army could come blow us up, and we'd all go out in a fiery hell-blaze of mindless togetherness. Just me and my zombies.

If only I had the courage, I said to no one in particular.

I buried my head in my lap. Tears soaked my jeans as I thought about my own inevitable death.

Then I heard a voice.

"Look up."

It was Cokie. It was her ghost, or a vision that my mind had made up. She stood before me in full battle dress, wearing the gleaming, metal-plated armor and helmet of a samurai.

I rubbed my eyes. Maybe I was going crazy. Maybe none of this was real.

"You're not really Cokie," I said. "You can't be. I saw you die."

"You can't win the game until you save the princess," Ghost Cokie said.

"What princess?" I really *was* losing my mind.

She held her finger to her lips as if to say, *Shhhh,* then pointed to the door behind me before fading away.

I rubbed my eyes again and blacked out.

20

A TUG ON THE LEG of my jeans brought me slowly awake.

"Cokie?" I mumbled through closed eyes.

More tugs, then I heard whispers. *Hey, get up,* the voice said. *Fun Hater, get up already.*

I forced my eyes open, and tried to sit up. As my vision came into focus, I saw a girl kneeling before me. Her hair was a tangled blonde nest, the kind of mess a rat would be proud to call home. Rivers of black mascara trailed down her face. Her dress was soiled, torn, and spattered with blood. Her shoes were long gone, leaving her bare feet to get black, exposing cherry-red toenails to the ravages of chipping. She was my life's nemesis, the one woman who plagued my pre-zombie days at every turn: Lila.

I gawked for a few seconds, shocked that she was still alive. Then I threw my arms around her legs and started to cry again.

"Sweet mother of a monkey. It's *you*," I squeaked, actually glad to see her.

"Come on," she urged, helping me up.

"Where are we going?" I managed to ask through my tears.

"To the video room, for now."

She spun me around. The door to the video room was right behind where I had passed out, the same spot Ghost Cokie had pointed to. Maybe she'd been trying to tell me something, that Lila and I would need each other for survival. Cokie was so much smarter than I had ever given her credit for.

Lila opened the door to the video room, helped me hobble inside, then shut the door behind us.

Video monitors played in every corner of the room, flickering black and white images of scenes from all over the school. My blood became ice: I saw nothing but creeps wandering the halls or feasting on bodies, heads down in guts and up to their elbows in gore.

Jesus, I muttered.

Lila looked at me solemnly. "I know."

"How on Earth are you getting this footage? And *why?*" I asked.

Lila shook her head, as if the answer was obvious. Then I realized that the answer *was* obvious. Lila had a history of secretly filming students and teachers, trying to catch them in nefarious deeds, then posting the videos online as part of her notorious gossip rag. Except that tonight she had outdone herself, and had placed hidden cameras everywhere in some extreme prom night exposé, looking to record students and teachers in compromising positions. Instead, Lila caught the disaster as it unfolded, wherever she had managed to sneak a camera. I felt sick to my stomach and turned my head, then saw two bodies splayed out on the other side of the room: Camera Boy and Sound Dude, both with their heads gashed open. And a bloody microphone pole on the floor. Lila had speared their skulls with it.

"Oh my God," I said. *Ohmygod-ohmygod-ohmygod!*

"I had to do it. They tried to eat me," Lila moaned.

I ran to the corner and vomited green bile, steadying myself against the wall with my hands. Lila began to cry, making sounds like a wounded animal. I wiped my mouth on my sleeve and came back to where she had slumped into a chair. I spotted her tiara, where it had been flung to a far corner of the room. A small video camera rested on the table, and the contents of a purse had exploded on the floor. Lip gloss, hairspray, eyeliner, cell phone—all the ingredients of a normal girl's prom night. But this night had been anything but normal.

Lila started whimpering. "Why…why is this happening… on this night, of all nights…I *swear* God is punishing us…" She was one *oy vey* short of tearing her hair out and ending it all. The one night she had been waiting for all her life—prom night—ruined by the unthinkable: zombies. It made me think of Cokie again. I missed her like crazy and there was no way to get her back. I shook my head and started to cry yet again, even though I didn't think I had a drop left in my body.

Lila looked up at me through her tears. "Look at us. We're two crying fools."

"I'm sorry," I said as I sat on the floor. "I just can't get over that I just watched my best friend kill herself. I don't think I'll *ever* get over it."

"I know…I saw it all on camera. I'm sorry…I'm so, so sorry," she said.

We both sat crying, completely overcome by everything that had happened. I stared from afar at the screens flickering on the wall, watching more destruction unfold in the school. Sadness and hopelessness soon gave way to something else, an anger that welled inside of me. I couldn't take it anymore, this thing called "two girls crying." It was bullshit. This wasn't what I was raised to do. My mom didn't raise me to sit in a room, blubbering over zombies and the supposed end of days. She didn't raise me to wait for a bomb to drop. No, my mom raised me to take charge, despite the worst that could happen, best friend dead or not. And that's what I was going to do. I stood up. "We need to stop crying, pull on our Big Girl Pants, and get the hell out of here. Do you know what's going on out there? I mean, in the city?"

She nodded. "I was up here when the whole thing went

down, and saw it on the news."

"So you know there's a chance the school might get torched?"

"Yes," she whispered.

"Then why don't you leave with me?"

"It was one thing to handle Camera Boy and Sound Dude when they came after me, but I don't know if I have it in me to face the rest of them. Besides, why should I live? What difference does it make to you if I get eaten or if I get blown up? How do we even know our families are safe, or that the world out there isn't totally screwed? They stopped broadcasting the news, all the stations went black. We can't use the phones. If we escape, we might not even have a reason to live."

"Well, I promised my best friend I'd rescue people tonight, and that includes you, because that's what she would have done, and because that's what her dad would have done. Her dad was a cop and was killed downtown, but she still kept going, until she died."

"Yeah, but Cokie killed herself," Lila mumbled.

"She killed herself because she got bit and didn't want to turn. She didn't want to become a liability."

"Maybe we should kill ourselves anyway."

"Trust me, I already thought about it."

"Then why don't we?"

"No way, I need to keep going."

"Then go without me."

"No."

"Jesus-Effing-Christ, Clarissa, it's not like we're suddenly best friends or anything. I should do what I want to do. It's my life. Or death, actually. So back the hell off."

I leaned in, pointing my finger at her chest where she sat in her chair. "Then why did you come get me? Why did you wake me up in the hall? You could have just left me alone and I would have left without you."

She got up, and handed me the little video camera from the table.

"What's this?" I asked.

"It's my last testament. Take it with you, in case you survive. And if my folks are alive, tell them I'm sorry."

I shook my head. "Geez, Lila."

"Don't blame me for how I feel. When I saw everything go down, I wanted to document my last night on Earth, and leave a message for anyone who survives. I told my family I missed them, and said I was sorry for turning into a Promzilla today, hogging the bathroom, accusing my sister of hiding my tiara, and being a psycho-meanie to anyone who got in my way. And I apologized to anyone I've ever stepped on, smeared, manipulated, and bitch-slapped. And you, I even apologized to you, if you want to know. Take this. I want everyone to know that Lila Logan had a change of heart and wasn't a total bi-yatch on the night she died."

I looked at her, incredulous. Not because I didn't believe that she'd had a change of heart, but because I wouldn't leave without her.

"Please?" she begged. "Come on! Of all nights to be a buzz-kill!"

"This isn't like you, Lila. You don't strike me as someone who'd give up. You never have. Even though we've never gotten along, you've always struck me as someone who knows how to beat the game. At all times."

She bit her lip. "Shit, just stop sweet-talking me. Seriously, just stop already and let me die."

"Remember the time you snuck back into school during parent-teacher conferences and caught some rich kid's dad bribing Mr. Wallingford for good grades? Just flashing his cash all over the place. Then you put the video online for the whole world to see. The local news picked up the story and Mr. Wally got fired for his ethical choices, but I have to admit, it was totally the right thing to do."

"Yeah, that was pretty epic." The corner of her mouth began to shift upward in a tiny smirk.

"Or how about the time you volunteered to help the janitor 'clean' the teacher's lounge, so you could plant a camera there, then you broadcasted a live feed into the cafeteria at lunch the next day, so all the kids could hear the nasty things teachers say behind our backs. Teacher-student relations were pretty bad for a few weeks, but *I* was okay because I hadn't been personally mentioned."

"That was a pretty good one too," Lila said.

"And there was the time you caught…"

Lila cut me off. "You're right, I've done some pretty bad-ass things with my life so far. Thanks for the pep talk." She crossed her arms against her chest, then narrowed her eyes, pressing her lips in a tight, thin line.

"So are you coming with me?"

She sighed. "Promise me you know what you're doing."

I thought about Cokie's gun, and the laser. I wouldn't shoot the gun, but I could totally rock the laser. "I've got just the method for getting us through the school unharmed."

Lila attempted a smile. "I think you're my new best friend."

I grinned.

"So what's your plan, woman?"

I explained the gun, and how Cokie had taken it from Taylor after he tried to kill us and we stopped him. And I explained how she used the laser to blind the zombies and stop them in their tracks so we could move through the school.

"Bad-ass. I think I saw her doing it on the monitor," she said. "So you know how to do it?"

"I think so."

"Not good enough, girlfriend. I need promises. Guarantees. This is my life we're talking about, remember?"

"I'm glad to see you value your life again. And, yes, I *know* I can handle the laser."

"That's so much better. So, where's this hot little pistol?"

"It's outside, by Cokie's body."

Lila jumped out of her chair. "Then let's grab it and go. But first, let's look at the monitors." She pulled me to the wall of screens. "This will help us figure out where to go next."

I scanned each one as the images flickered from hallway to classrooms. Truth was, I couldn't see any survivors. I couldn't believe my eyes. I stared longer, hoping to prove myself wrong.

"Look there." Lila pointed to the screen showing the library, where a lone boy ran for his life, dodging other boys in plain clothes who had gone crazy and were out for blood.

I squinted, trying to look closer. I couldn't recognize him, but remembered Cokie's words from when we were holed up in the teacher's lounge: *Just keep an open mind. You don't know who's out there. Maybe…maybe there's someone you haven't given a chance yet.*

"And look, *there,*" Lila pointed to another screen, grasping my arm so hard with her other hand that her nails dug into my skin.

My blood froze as I caught a boy walking in the front office. I couldn't make out his face, but could make out the shape of his jacket. A military jacket. And a big black gun hanging by his side. Cokie had been wrong. Taylor was alive, awake, and probably *totally* pissed.

Oh, shit.

Shit, shit, shit!

21

MY STOMACH TWISTED into knots as I watched Taylor on the monitor. He picked up the intercom microphone just as Cokie and I had done over an hour ago, and his voice boomed from the speaker above. "Clarissa Hargrove and Cokie Morimoto, and anyone who's still alive: your time is up, bitches. I'm coming to find you. That is, *we* are coming to find you, me and my big, bad gun. And while I make my way through the school, I'm going to shoot all these fucking zombies. If *you* ladies have turned into zombies, Clarissa and Cokie, then that's fucking great, because I'll be doing you a favor by ending you. Whatever. I'm getting out of here alive and people will call me a motherfucking hero."

Before I realized what was happening, Lila darted to the intercom and pressed the button. "Fuck you, Tay—"

I ran over and swatted her hand off it. "What the hell! Don't you know he can tell where we are now? The intercom shows the zones of the school, with little orange lights showing where the call came from. He totally knows we're down here now."

Her eyes went wide. "Oh, shit...I am so sorry! I am so, so, sorry!"

Taylor's voice thundered over the intercom again. "Well, well, well. Hello, ladies. It appears I've now got some survivors to take care of. Do you need taking care of, girls? Looks like you're downstairs? Music and media zone? No need to answer that. The little orange lights have told me everything. See you soon, bitches...and I hope you've said your prayers. You're really going to need them." Feedback shrilled over the intercom, then we heard a click, and the transmission ended.

We ran back to the monitor, trying to come to grips with what just happened. My lungs squeezed as I watched him leave the office and start firing on the zombies in his path, their bodies rattling under a storm of bullets.

"Oh fuck..." Lila said. "Oh, FUCK." She began to shake, and breathed hard like she was about to hyperventilate. I needed to help her stay in control, or we'd be doomed.

"Okay, if we stay calm, we can figure out what to do, and be safe. We need to be one step ahead of him, so we won't be down here when he gets here. Once we get out of this sound-proof room, we'll hear his gun going off, so we'll know he's coming. We just have to pray our paths won't cross. And we'll try to get out from another part of the school."

She shook even harder. "I don't know if this is a good idea."

I grabbed both her shoulders and looked her dead in the eyes. "I'm scared too, but if we hide, he'll keep looking until he finds us, then he'll kill us anyway. I don't see any other choice but to run. We can stay alive if we stick together. So let's hurry, okay?"

She nodded, breathing more slowly, and deeply.

I handed her my bat. "Do you know what to do with this?"

She composed herself and nodded again, glancing over at the bodies of Camera Boy and Sound Dude in the corner. "I handled those guys, remember?"

"That's my girl. Let's go."

22

AS WE LEFT the video room, I was more freaked out than I let on. One false move, one tiny miscalculation, and we'd be shredded. All my efforts to survive so far would be wasted. The truth was, I'd rather be eaten by zombies than let Taylor take us down. I tried to hide my shaking. Then I noticed Lila's cast-off tiara again, and felt sad that she wouldn't need it anymore. I wished we could go back in time and erase everything that happened, and that she could still be prom queen, because that's what she wanted. I made a mental note: if we lived through tonight, I'd crown her honorary prom queen. I was sure she would like that.

We ran to Cokie's and Connor's bodies in the hall, and I tried not to focus on the fact that my best friend was lying there, dead, or I'd lose my last bit of sanity. I bent down and picked up Cokie's gun, and studied it, remembering how to press the button to activate the laser. The beam shot out before us, and Lila exhaled with relief. We were on our way.

We dashed up the rest of the hall, under flickering lightbulbs and up the stairs to the main floor. My hair stood on end as the sound of Taylor's gunshots rang through the school. I pushed the fear out of my mind, and cracked the door open to peek down the next hall and make sure Taylor wasn't visible. But I saw something else: creeps and munchers, some disintegrating and moving slow, others more intact and moving faster.

"Oh, God." Lila said. "They're hideous."

"Shhhhh," I whispered. I needed to focus, to summon all my energy toward getting us down there alive. I steadied my arms as I raised the pistol, aiming the laser at the eyes of the closest ones. They yowled and fell, some swiping at their eyes with their hands, others flailing the stumps of their limbs. I let the air out of my lungs, feeling a surge of relief and pride that I knocked them over with just a laser. In fact, I felt pretty bad-ass. *Cokie, wherever you are, I bet you'd high-five me right now.*

I stepped from behind the stairwell door and started to move, motioning for Lila to follow. She came out, moving cautiously at first, but then picked up the pace as we wove around the thrashing monsters.

I had made it past them when Lila screamed behind me. I whirled around. She had tripped over the ragged edges of her gown, sending her bat flying. Two sightless creeps in tattered tuxes crawled toward her from behind, gnashing their teeth as she scrambled to get away. She tumbled again, this time landing on top of a bloody zombie girl who wore the same dress as she did. They wrestled as Lila wailed for help, holding the zombie's head at arm's length to keep from being bitten.

I panicked. I didn't want to use the laser *or* fire the gun, fearing I'd compromise or even kill Lila by accident. I tucked the pistol back in my pants, then retrieved Lila's bat. When I had a chance at a good swing and was sure I wouldn't injure Lila, I smashed at the zombie girl's legs. She howled, loosening her grip on my friend, who hustled to get up. Then we both darted away.

"Fuck, that was crazy," she panted as she ran beside me.

"I know. Welcome to my world."

Lila clutched my arm as the stream of *rat-a-tat* gunfire got louder and startled us dead in our tracks.

"He's getting closer," I said.

Lila's eyes got wider. "Ohmygosh, where do we go?"

Out of nowhere, Ghost Cokie materialized down the hall, standing before the cafeteria in her samurai gear. She raised her arm and pointed to the door.

"The nearest exit is through the cafeteria," I said. "We need to get there before we run into Taylor. Hurry."

We sprinted again, the sound of Lila's bare feet slapping the linoleum between the sound of approaching gunshots. We ran almost to the end of the hall, but I stopped us right behind the corner, ten feet away from the lunchroom. I didn't want us to run right into the fray, I wanted to see what was coming first. I peeked around the edge of the wall; there was no sign of Taylor. But the gunfire kept moving closer, and I heard shouting. My breath caught in my throat at the sound of Taylor's maniacal voice.

"I've got you, zombie motherfuckers, *I've got you!* Don't even *think* that I won't blow your *fucking* heads off. Oh wait, you're zombies. You *can't* think. Poor little zombies."

More shots blasted out.

"POOR. LITTLE. ZOMBIES!"

"He's almost here," Lila hissed. *"Let's-go-let's-go-let's-go!"*

We bolted out from behind the corner, making a mad dash for the cafeteria. Lila was about to press open the doors, but I blocked her with my arm, because my laser had shut off. The zombies from the cafeteria were still inside, and the ones that had fallen behind us in the hall were due to get back up. I kept pressing the laser's "on" button, but it didn't work. The battery must have died, or maybe a screw was loose like before. *Shit.*

Just then Taylor rounded the corner, spotted us, and roared. *"Stop right there, bitches!"*

We froze in place. This was most certainly the end.

23

WE SPUN TO face him. I shoved the gun in my pants and Lila dropped her bat. We put our hands in the air, and Lila started to whimper. My gut twisted in knots again. I didn't want either of us to die.

Taylor kept his rifle trained on us as he moved closer. "Geez, Lila," he shouted. "Just shut the fuck up already, you fucking crybaby. And you, Clarissa—where's your little friend Cokie?" he sneered. "Because I want to fuck her up *first*."

I stood there shivering, my anxiety threatening to win and render me completely useless. But I wasn't going to die without at least telling Taylor that Cokie was a hero. "She died trying to save kids," I said, which was mostly true. Then I started to remember how she really died, and couldn't stop the tears from streaming down my face.

"Aw, poor baby. I know, this is so *scary*, isn't it? You lost your little slave—I mean your best friend—trying to save all those kids. How crazy is it that every one of those dumb fucks turned into zombies, huh? And you were so *hell-bent* on saving them, but it looks like prom got them anyway. Now I get to do what I've always wanted to do—turn this school into target practice. Isn't this gun a beauty, by the way? Semi-automatic. Built to shred people." He pointed it in the air, and shot it around in a semicircle, shattering light fixtures and shredding the ceiling to bits in a spray of bullets. We hit the floor, covering our ears with our hands as Taylor laughed. Sparks zapped in all directions.

"Well, guess what?" he continued. "I'm going to finish what I started. Then I'll escape as the last person alive, and I'll tell everyone I *had* to kill you, because you were both zombies, and then I'll be a hero. How does that sound, bitches?"

He pointed the rifle at me first.

Lila whimpered louder. "Don't kill her. Please don't kill her."

I froze where I lay on the ground, feeling sicker than ever. My mouth felt like straw and every inch of my body trembled. I had come so far, only to die like *this?*

"Taylor, please...you are better than this," I begged. "Just because some of those kids were assholes doesn't mean you are. You can walk outta here and everything can be different. I promise you. Please...it's not too late. Just put your gun down and leave with us."

I saw a flicker of sorrow in his eyes. He clenched his jaw again, and his nose began to run like he might cry.

"Please, Taylor. Please."

He shook his head violently. "You're wrong, it *is* too late. I have *nothing* to live for. *Nothing!* I might as well take everyone down with me. So shut up, bitch. This is goodbye."

He peered through the sight, about to squeeze the trigger. I closed my eyes. This was really, really the end.

There was a click, then nothing.

I opened my eyes. Taylor pressed the trigger again. *Click.*

"Fuck," he said, stomping the floor. "FUCK. I wasted my last round on a vanity shot."

Then I did what any self-respecting girl would do when given a second chance.

"Nobody calls me bitch," I said.

I grabbed the bat from the floor, scrambled to my knees and swung it, smashing his kneecaps. *Thwack!*

Taylor fell to the ground, screaming in pain. I swung at his legs again and again and again, just to make sure he stayed down.

"You crazy bitch!" he screamed. *"Why don't you just kill me?! Because if you let me live, you'll regret it the rest of your living days!"*

"Oh, I'm not going to let you live," I said, clutching the bat hard. "Mostly because you called me bitch again. When are you ever going to learn?"

I was bluffing. *Of course* I was going to let him live. I'm a pacifist, mostly. But I didn't know what to do next with that crazy motherfucker. I knew that time was of the essence and that anything could happen.

Nights like this teach you at least that much.

24

LILA AND I both stepped back, giving Taylor space while I racked my brains for our next move. A timid she-monster shuffled around the corner, dragging the raw stump of a foot that poked out from a tattered and blood-soaked pink gown. It was StumpGirl from before. She wobbled forward as slow, raspy breaths scraped from her throat. Her eyes shone with a new level of wildness, a hunger more alive than I'd seen all night. Her lips twitched and her nostrils flared, sniffing as though she had been chasing a scent, something familiar that caused her to lick her lips and growl.

I stared, straining to remember who she was in real life, her other life, before she became a zombie.

Recognition stung me. It was Christie McIntire—Taylor's ex—the girl he had plotted to kill tonight, along with everyone else.

She ignored us and stumbled toward Taylor, who still moaned on the floor. More creeps followed, until a crowd of ghouls pressed around him. Taylor laughed and screamed at the same time.

"That is just PERFECT!" he shouted. "THANK YOU, karma!"

They swarmed over him in a frenzy, holding his body down, growling as they ripped him apart with their teeth. His screams grew to a crescendo, then slowed to a low gurgle and stopped, silenced forever by the horde.

We stood behind the fray, staring and speechless, not believing that they had chosen him over us. Horrified, we kept watching while they gorged, face down in his organs, intestines hanging from their mouths as they bathed in his blood. It wasn't safe to stay, yet here we were, unable to move, unable to look away from the show. What we learned in school was true: nature was violent and cruel, but always took care of its own.

Thank you, karma, I thought. *Thank you so much.*

STANDING THERE, I remembered that a lone boy was still trapped in the library—that is, if he was even still alive—and I searched my soul for the strength to pull off my next move, to find and maybe even rescue a potential new friend. I tugged at Lila's arm to drag us both away from the spectacle, and let the creeps finish their work without us.

Alerted by our movement, they looked up and stared at us, rearing their heads one by one, like grotesque blood-soaked meerkats.

"Ruuuuuuuuuuun," I shouted, then bolted in the direction of the library, trying not to be grossed out by the bodies and gore as I ran past.

"Where are we going?" Lila screeched, trailing behind me. "I thought our exit was back that way!"

"There's one last kid in the library, we saw him on the video monitors!"

"Oh yeah! Let's get him!"

We ran about thirty paces until we reached the library door. I peered in through the side window, a wall of glass that surrounded the library. I couldn't see anything from where I was standing. On the video monitors less than fifteen minutes ago, I had seen the boy running away from the zombies, heading toward the fiction stacks, endless rows of bookshelves. I prayed that somewhere in there, he was still alive.

I took stock of my weapons. I still had my baseball bat, but the gun's laser had stopped working. As for using the gun itself, I didn't know the first thing about shooting one, and would have killed myself if I tried. I'd have to be strong and finish this fight the old-fashioned way. If I had to, I'd swing, remembering what

Cokie told me about piñatas.

"When we go in there, stay behind me," I told Lila. "Or feel free to hide behind the librarian's desk to stay safe."

"Hell no. I'm helping. Like I want you to get all the credit for being bad-ass tonight."

"Glad you came around."

I opened the door and bounded down the stairs into the library, Lila right behind me. She grabbed a chair, holding it up like a lion tamer. I gripped my bat so hard it should have splintered in my hands.

"Hey, zombies, come out, come out, wherever you are," I called out in a sing-song voice from the open space in the library. "And leave that kid alone!"

Five monsters scrambled out from between the stacks, snarling as they charged at us. Something in me snapped when I saw their faces, the wild yet vacant stares. Though they were once kids, their humanity was long gone, and they now played for the wrong team. The people-eater team. And I wasn't going to take it anymore, non-violent principles be damned. I ran forward to meet them, screaming primally from the depths of my being, voicing the rage of a thousand teenage vegans, and swung hard, smashing one skull, then another, and another, and another, all of them screeching as they dropped. Lila ran twenty feet, ramming her chair through the air and pinning the fifth zombie against the wall through its eye socket, the way she had killed Camera Boy and Sound Dude with the microphone pole. She let go of the chair and the creep tumbled to the carpet.

We poked at their bodies to make sure they were dead, then we stopped, gasping for air as we took in the mess, the brains of the boy's nerdy ex-friends spattered across a display of the classics: *Lord of the Flies, Heart of Darkness, Fahrenheit 451*. My mind reeled. I couldn't believe I was a zombie killer. But when another human being is in danger—whether they're your friend or not—it blinds you to all logic, and you do what you thought was impossible. It was the same thing that drove Cokie to save Connor. The same force that helps moms to lift two-ton cars off their trapped children. The same energy that makes you bash zombie heads when you have to, like I did.

I barely heard a wavering voice calling out from somewhere behind the stacks.

My heart leaped. The boy was alive.

We ran toward the fiction stacks, scanning past each one. We found the study area at the back, where chairs had been thrown, knocked over and smashed, and a pile of study desks had been haphazardly turned over to make an impromptu fort.

"Hello?" I called out.

Eyes peered from an opening in the desk fort.

"Are you okay?" I asked.

He nodded, but otherwise didn't move.

"Do you need a hand getting out of there?" Lila asked.

"There's no one else here in the library but us, so you're totally safe to come out," I added.

He squinted. "Are you sure you're not zombies?" he called out. "I mean, how do I know?"

"We're sure, dude," Lila said. "Just trust us already."

"Only if you pass this test. Count backward, in odd numbers only, from nineteen to one."

Lila and I looked at each other. This kid was a piece of work, but he had a point. I had to prove that I was still a thinking human, and not a mindless people-eater.

"Fine, I'll do it," I said. I rattled off the odd numbers starting with nineteen, ending all the way at one. Lila rolled her eyes the whole time.

"Okay, you passed," he said. "Now you, Lila."

She sighed loudly then counted backwards the way I had done.

"Great, you both passed. Now, help me out."

Lila and I started pulling the desks apart from each other, and the boy groaned as he collapsed flat on the carpet from where he had scrunched himself up to hide. It was Jaime Jonsson, one of the boys in my Ethics and Philosophy class—a nice, quiet kid I had never given the time of day to. He was dressed in street clothes, not prom clothes. Then I looked around, curious, noticing scattered game boards and game pieces, and a crumpled sign that said, *Anti-Prom Game Night. All are welcome.* I felt a twinge in my chest, sad that I hadn't noticed the same signs around the school in the weeks before prom. Jaime and I had been two ships passing in the night.

He sat up. I held out my hand to help him stand, and he looked embarrassed. He hesitated, first taking off his cracked Buddy Holly glasses to wipe them on his shirt, then hastily wiped his reddened face on his sleeve, pretending he hadn't been crying at some point. I sighed. Typical guy behavior. Then he finally slipped his hand into mine, and Lila offered hers too, and we yanked him up.

"Thanks," he said, his voice cracking as he came to his feet. He was shaking, almost hyperventilating, and struggled to pull an inhaler out of his pants pocket. He took a puff before shoving it back and resuming his shaking. He looked around, scanning the room like he expected something to jump out any second now. "Are you sure it's just you guys?"

"We're sure," I said, fighting back tears as I remembered that Cokie wasn't with us anymore. "We'll explain everything later. We just really, really need to go."

He nodded, and the three of us started making our way to the front of the library, careful not to step on any books that had been knocked down in the fray. Something in this crazy world had to be kept sacred.

We looked up, startled by pounding noises, and stopped in our tracks. More creeps stood at the window—a wall of them.

They looked worse than ever, their tuxes and gowns more shredded than before, their faces more mangled, more eyes, noses, and ears missing, torn or gouged right from their heads. The occasional missing foot or hand left behind only the raw stump of a limb. And gore covered their bodies, leaving red smears against the wall of glass. The sight raised every hackle on my body, and every muscle froze; every beat of my heart threatened imminent cardiac arrest. But there'd be no ambulance tonight, no emergency medical rescue team. Getting out of here alive? That would be solely up to me.

Before I could think out my next move, the window shattered, and most of the horde tumbled into the room under a blitz of tiny glass daggers.

"Ruuuuuuuuuuuuuuuuuuuuuuuuuun," I yelled, rushing up the stairs toward the library door. I yanked it open and ran through with Lila and Jaime behind me. We bolted for the front exit, another fifty paces away. More zombies moaned down the hall behind us, shuffling and lurching after our young, fresh meat. We needed to bust out of there.

I screeched to a halt right before the exit, and poised my bat high above my head, hoping to break the zip ties that clamped the school shut.

"Hurry!" Lila urged. "They're getting closer!"

I took a deep breath, summoning every ounce of remaining strength, and envisioned myself as a samurai like Cokie. I swung the bat down hard, but missed, smashing the floor instead. I swore under my breath.

"They're coming up right behind us," Jaime warned.

I swung again, hitting the zip tie but only managing to stretch it under the impact.

Then I tried a third time. *Wherever you are, Cokie, this is for you.*

The zip tie snapped and fell to the ground.

"Go, go, go!" Lila hollered, pushing open the door. We hurried through and slammed it shut behind us, a blast of cool air and mist hitting our faces in the moonlit night. We ran down the cement stairs and tumbled to the wet sidewalk in a heap.

I sat up and clung to Jaime's arm, bursting into tears, not believing that we had survived. He pulled me closer, then pulled in Lila too. We huddled together, shivering on the ground and catching our breath, thankful that no zombies were immediately in sight.

I looked up at the sky. The military was supposed to come, to nuke the school the way they had torched others on television. A glance at my watch revealed that hours had gone by since the ordeal began. I scanned the street in front of the school and scanned the horizon, seeing plumes of smoke as I listened for sounds of helicopters, sirens, ambulances, anything.

Nothing.

The world was eerily quiet. The moon had risen high in the

sky. I let go of my new friends and stood up to check the fields where I had seen the monsters roaming before, when I looked through the windows at the back of the school. I started walking toward the hill to get a better view.

"Where are you going?" Jaime called out, rushing beside me to catch up.

"Yeah, where do you think you're going? We're a team now, you can't just go anywhere without us," Lila sniffled, following too.

I smiled in spite of all that had happened, grateful for Lila's friendship. "There's something I've gotta see," I told her.

"Well, we're coming with you," Jaime said.

He bumped into my side as we walked, and I snuck a surreptitious sideways glance. His eyes were blue, a dreamier blue than Mr. Harrison's, and I sure had a thing for blue ones. My heart skipped a beat, something we called *paroxysmal supraventricular tachycardia* in Biology class. Our gaze met, and Jaime blushed and looked down, flashing a quick smile that he tried to hide. He had mouthful of shiny metal braces, and they were beautiful.

"Geez," Lila whispered in my ear. "You guys aren't doing the icky teen romance thing already, are you? I mean, we just escaped a meat grinder and all you can think about is your first date. Seriously, just stop already. It's really inappropriate, we need to concentrate on other things..." she jabbed me in the ribs.

Lila was right, but I couldn't control myself. I walked even closer to Jaime, and felt myself blushing hard back at him. I'd never blushed that much at a boy before, because I didn't think feminists could do that, but I had to admit: just this once, it felt really, really nice.

We crested the hill overlooking the fields behind the school. I felt a heavy sadness at what I saw. The monsters were still there, stumbling in the mud and grass over and over again, wandering aimlessly under the moon. I couldn't make out their faces, but said a silent prayer for all the kids whose names I could remember, to honor who they were, before their lives, as they knew them, had ended. Herman Johnson, star basketball player; Tina Minari, budding film director; Thelma Kane, animal lover; Angel Barton, blues singer; Royden Jones, graffiti artist; Chloe Tisch, young fashion critic; Brian Beeson, future economist; Lukas Wilde, up-and-coming actor; Hannah Berg, megawatt cheerleader; Rajini Prajiv, aspiring astronaut. And more, and more, and more.

Suddenly, I spotted something new in the center of the field, glinting under the stadium lights. A figure in metal-plated armor and a samurai helmet stood, waiting for my attention. She lifted up her sword and pointed it at me, then swashed at the air around her before bowing deeply in my direction as a sign of respect.

Cokie.

She faded away as soon as I'd seen her, and I wiped away one last tear. *Thank you for teaching me to be brave.*

My new friends and I stood side by side, staring at the fields in silence. I felt super lucky to have them, and drew them both in closer. Then I dug my hand into the pocket of my gore-crusted jeans, fished out the keys to my Volvo, and jingled them in the air.

"Let's go."

We had no idea what lay ahead, but we were together. And in the end, that's all that mattered.

EPILOGUE

IT'S BEEN MORE than a year since the outbreak. The virus was ultimately traced back to a shipment of Grade E government-surplus hotdogs, which had been delivered to government buildings, senior centers, and public schools around the country—including my high school. The offending sick-dogs were served forty-eight hours before prom, just enough time to incubate and cause the prom night disaster. But the kids and teachers at my school ate lunch in shifts—lunch period one, period two and period three—resulting in waves of onset of the illness, not to mention varying levels of disintegration. I never got sick because I'm a vegan, *natch*, and Cokie always ate the bento box lunches her mom lovingly packed. Lila had an eating disorder, and had been purging her food more than usual that week to help her squeeze into that rib-crushing, boob-enhancing prom dress. Last, but not least, the mystery meat never once crossed Jaime's lips because he had severe food allergies, and had to stay away from anything pre-packaged or not homemade for fear of hidden ingredients that made his windpipe swell shut. Since we've started dating, I can't tell you how many times I've had to jab that boy with an EpiPen. Seriously. It's crazy.

More kids survived that night, like the stoners who ate nothing but chips or brownies for lunch and didn't even care about prom. They had stayed home and smoked pot in their basements, and were safe. Or at least that's what the rumors say. When I heard this, I laughed. Everyone always said that stoners would amount to nothing in this world, but it turns out they were among the few who survived. At least the first wave of zombie attacks, anyway. I'd still never smoke pot though. I've heard it dulls your reflexes, and trust me, I've learned a lot about needing quick reflexes. And too many brownies make you too fat to run. I know this now.

Otherwise, proms and playgrounds everywhere became the scenes of living nightmares, with unsuspecting teens and young innocent children in training pants and pigtails developing an insatiable yearning for human flesh. I had always known, in a way, that America's youth were fucked, but I hadn't thought it would go down the way it did. As for our senior citizens,

I imagined rabid elderly people tripping over their walkers during prime time television to get a taste of each other, their soft, crepe-paper skin giving way under Chiclet dentures. I shudder every time I think about it.

Even our military had eaten the tainted meat, which is why no one came to bomb the school that night. Soldiers started to get sick as the night wore on, resulting in a useless army of zombies, so no help arrived for days, leaving the infection to spread. After about four days' time, Canadian Special Forces invaded the U.S., cordoning off and torching open spaces and buildings with a known mass quantity of the infected. After a few long months, the outbreak was largely contained, but not before ending America's career as a world super power. In fact, the U.S. is now the U.P.O.C.—the United Provinces of Canada. As ironic as this seems, we have better health care in a time when we need it most, and that's no joke.

Some of the infected escaped in those first few days, and took off wandering the hills and woods. Sometimes, one or two will emerge from the forest, looking for their next meal with dazed, sunken eyes and purple flesh hanging off their bones. Most people in my neighborhood have learned to shoot guns, so zombies rarely have a chance anymore. Me? I still think guns suck. But I've started taking archery lessons and hope to rock a pretty hot crossbow some day, which I plan to use strictly for zombies, if the need should ever arise. And I'm still pretty good with a bat. So don't you worry about me. I'll be just fine.

Back at home, Dad had come to see the folly of his meat-eating ways. Feeling lucky that he had avoided tainted meat at home because Mom always bought locally-sourced organic food, Dad still worried that he'd dodged a bullet, because he sometimes ate at the I.R.S. cafeteria where he worked. So he became vegan, like me. Now we high-five each other in the kitchen as we prepare our nightly supper, using whatever vegan food source we can muster. And though I've learned to make tastier vegan dishes, thanks to Dad, Mom still turns up her nose at whatever we make. Between you and me, despite my dad's progress at renouncing meat, I once found him in the basement, relapsing into addict behavior, practically snorting a dusty container of bacon bits that he'd found at the back of the pantry. Some things never change.

As for Cokie, I miss her like crazy. I never saw Ghost Cokie again, probably because she had taught me all I needed to know. But Lila had stepped up to the plate, and we became the unlikeliest of best friends. Sure, we still argue a lot, about whether or not feminists should or shouldn't wear makeup, and whether or not we should have sold our story to the mass media, who declared me a Vegan Teenage Zombie Huntress, with my blood-spattered face screaming from the front pages of the tabloids—even though it wasn't quite the truth. Movie and book offers pour in from the remaining dregs of Hollywood and New York, and I'm trying to figure out how to deal with it. I'm just glad that things are sort of back to normal. Even if paparazzi hound us at every turn.

So what else is new, you ask? Oh yeah, Jaime and I got a dog. A zombie-hunting, zombie-sniffing dog, with a patch of black over one eye. She stiffens and growls whenever she spots someone walking with a slight limp or shuffle. Her training needs a little fine-tuning—she's almost bitten several disabled people when we walk past the neighborhood nursing home—but I always manage to call her off just in time. If and when the next zombie outbreak happens, this time we'll be ready for it. And I promise I'll be much, much braver.

[ALMOST, BUT NOT QUITE, THE END]

A JOURNALIST'S TELEVISION INTERVIEW WITH
CLARISSA AND LILA, 1 YEAR LATER

Interviewer: Clarissa, does your special zombie-fighting baseball bat have a name, and if so, what is it?

Clarissa: Yes, she does have a name, thanks for asking. Her name is Margaret Thatcher, for obvious reasons.

Interviewer: <laughs> That's great. It's a little nerdy, but great.

Clarissa: <scowls at interviewer> Don't call me nerdy.

Interviewer: Sorry. Ok, this next question is for both of you. How have recent events changed your attitude toward each other? Specifically, smart women often have trouble getting along. Are you collaborative or competitive?

Lila: We used to hate each other, quite frankly, but the zombie apocalypse taught us that we're more alike than we thought. We were two competitive independent young women who needed each other to survive. So we became collaborative. We're friends now. Best friends.

Clarissa: But that doesn't mean we don't fight.

Lila: Right.

Clarissa: It's more of a "respectful dialogue."

Lila: Meaning, we can't call each other bitch.

Clarissa: For the record, I never once called you bitch. *You* used to call *me* bitch.

Lila: Um, right. Sorry.

Interviewer: <clears throat> Ladies...next question, please. Obviously you're best friends now, but you used to be enemies. It's rumored, though, that many years before your high-school dislike for each other, you were best friends in first grade, before Clarissa took up with Cokie. Word on the street says there was an incident revolving around a type of doll with unrealistic beauty standards that caused you to break up. Please discuss.

Lila: <sighs> Ok, so we totally used to hang out when we were, like, six years old. But we split up because she cut the beautiful, long blonde hair off my dolls. Just chopped it all off with a scissor—snip, snip. I was really ticked off. She had no right.

Clarissa: Geez, I was only six. Let it go!

Lila: <sighs> It's hard to let it go. I really, really loved my dolls!

Clarissa: Toys are the patriarchy's first attempt at control.

Lila: Well, I *was* only six.

Clarissa: That's what I'm saying, it starts young.

Interviewer: It's quite clear that you don't agree on everything. What *do* you agree on?

Clarissa: We can use the media to change things.

Lila: Yeah.

Interviewer: Please elaborate.

Clarissa: By showing images of strong, healthy, empowered women in the media, we can show girls that they can do cool things. Big things.

Lila: Like curing cancer.

Clarissa: Or fighting zombies.

Lila: Yeah.

Interviewer: You ladies are great. I'm very much enjoying our time together.

Clarissa: It's not over yet.

Interviewer: Right. Ok, a few more questions. There are rumors you've sold the movie rights to your story. Is that true?

Clarissa: <whispers to Lila> Should we tell her?

Lila: I'll handle this. We've been in various talks with key players, and have come close to cutting a deal, though we won't sign with just anyone.

Interviewer: Please tell me more.

Clarissa: We won't sign unless a) the money is right, and b) it's with a female director who has a history of portraying women in strong roles.

Interviewer: Why so concerned with money?

Lila: It's important that women learn to ask for what they're worth.

Interviewer: How much are you worth?

Lila: The sky's the limit.

Clarissa: But it's not all about us. If we came into wealth, we'd share it. We'd fix stuff. We'd help people.

Interviewer: Of course. So tell me something else: there are also rumors about who could potentially be cast in the film. Any thoughts?

Clarissa: Whatever. Who cares. I just want the right talent. And I want the women to look real. Not like some Hollywood bimbo versions of us, with perfectly-styled hair and perfectly thin eyebrows. I mean, who really looks like that?

Lila: Yeah. Not everyone has to look like me, a gorgeous blonde chick. Like, that's so boring.

Interviewer: Ladies, I'm going to change the subject. Let's talk about Cokie, you must miss her.

Clarissa: <tears up>

Interviewer: That's OK. Take your time.

Clarissa: I think about her every day.

Interviewer: That must be hard.

Clarissa: It is. I try not to be too depressive. I just try to channel her awesomeness. Everyday, when faced with a difficult challenge, I ask myself, What would Cokie do?

Lila: Totally.

Interviewer: That's wonderful. <pauses> Ladies, we have time for one more question before we have to wrap this up. This one is for Clarissa. Do you want to talk about your love life?

Clarissa: No, I don't, actually. Why is it that when women are interviewed by mass media that people only care about our sex lives? And our hairstyles? And our makeup? No one wants to talk about our awesome achievements. But they should. We're more than just tits and baby-makers. We do the hard stuff. Just ask Hillary Clinton. She'll show you how it's done.

Lila: Good answer. That question was offensive. <To interviewer> You should be ashamed of yourself.

Clarissa: Yeah, this interview is done.

Lila: Clarissa, are you thinking what I'm thinking?

Clarissa: Yes. Do it.

Lila: <gets out of chair and knocks over camera, the image goes black>

TURN THE PAGE FOR A SNEAK PREVIEW
OF THE NEXT BOOK IN THE SERIES,

STONERS VS. MOANERS

STONERS VS. MOANERS

CHAPTER 1

Everyone says that stoners are losers—that we're dumb and worthless and we'll never amount to a hill of beans, but that couldn't be farther from the truth. I may not do much now, but I have an exceptionally high IQ, and I'm still trying to figure out what to do with my life. To my mom and dad, it looks like I've checked out, and maybe I have. Sort of. From school anyway.

Ok, so my grades suck. But school isn't about creating original thinkers. It's about creating monkeys in suits who nod their heads up and down for the boss when he asks them to bend over. It's for making zombies in white shirts who shuffle off to their sorry day jobs, slogging in traffic to pay taxes to The Man, who'll just send their kids off to the meat-grinder of war. No thanks. I don't want to be a cog in the machine. Seriously. Down with The System. I'd rather be a stoner. And I am—a dyed-in-the-wool, shoulda-been-born-in-the-60s stoner. Except I don't want to be a burnout. I want to be more than that. I want to change the world, some day. I don't know how, but I will. But first, I need to smoke a joint and think really, really hard. I wish Mike would hurry up with the goods. Christ, where is that kid?

My pocket's buzzing with a text message. It's gotta be Mike.

Wassup? Got yr stuff. I can still come over right?

Mike's my best friend, one of the few black kids at Redvale High, and the class valedictorian. His parents are rocket scientists. I'm not kidding—they really are. Everything's so easy for Mike—that nerd dreams in math symbols and speaks like Plato in debate club, and even got early acceptance to M.I.T. That's why no one suspects him of being a stoner, like me. Well played, Mike. Well played.

I text him back. Dude, bring it. What's taking u so long??

Tonight's prom night, but neither of us is going. Prom is for jocks and preps, and I'm neither. Prom's just another way for The Man to suck kids into The System. Plus, I hate top 40. I'd rather sit at home and listen to Floyd, and, well, you know.

"Joseph! Joe!" My mom calls my name down the stairs.

"What?"

"Don't forget you have to watch your little sister tonight!"

Oh God. It's my parents' monthly poker night. All their work buddies from the I.R.S. are coming over. So now I've got Ruby-duty, watching my pain-in-the-nuts little sister. She's a pain because she's something of an escape artist. You think I'm kidding, but I'm not. Houdini Jr. can barely speak complete sentences, but she has some real tricks. You can blink and somehow she'll be on another floor of the house, getting into something dangerous. Like that time I swear I turned my head for a second and she got into the garage and scaled my dad's shelves, climbing toward the saws. Or the time she not only crawled out of her crib, but also stripped off her clothes, tore off her diaper, unlocked the front door, and toddled down the street, stark naked and screaming with joy. The neighbors found her, and knocked on our front door, holding her under the armpits as they handed her back to me. It blew my freaking mind; it hadn't even been five minutes since I'd put her to bed. When my parents found out, they blamed me for not having eyes on every side of my head like some kind of mutant super-nanny, and went crazy Ruby-proofing the doors even more than they already were. We're talking triple layer baby-gate action, deadbolts, blah, blah, blah. Not that it's actually worked, because the kid can't be contained. It means she and I will be under lockdown together tonight. Which means we're going to be playing with absurdly oversexed dolls with pointy, torpedo-like boobs. It also means I can't smoke. Or swear.

Fuck.

Dude, change of plans. Ruby-duty.

I am a nice guy, and I hate it. I wish I was one of those kids who didn't care what his parents thought, and ran off to stay out late and live life in epic ways, but I'm not. The truth is, I'm a complete bull-shitter: all this talk about not being a sucker for The Man and I can't even stand up to my folks. I'm such a loser. A loser with a capital L.

I feel my pocket buzzing again.

Got u covered, man. Got something else for ya. U won't have 2 smoke it.

Good old Mike.

Dude, u rock.

"Joe!" Mom is calling down the stairs again.

"What now?"

"We're getting pizzas! What do you want?"

"An extra-large white pie with extra cheese, and extra conformity, please."

"What?! Extra cheese?"

Nobody ever gets my jokes.

"Yup, Ma. That'll do."

Half an hour goes by, and I hear the doorbell ring upstairs. I bet that's Mike, and he's probably already chatting up my dad.

He's got this thing about being extra respectful to parents so no one suspects you're a stoner. I think that's why I don't have the heart to talk back to my folks. Damn you, Mike, for turning me into the nicest of pussies.

I run up the stairs and into the living room, navigating around my little sister's annoying toys, which happen to be everywhere. I never had this many toys when I was a kid. That spoiled little shit. One of these days, I'm going to break my neck, tripping over a giant hunk of pink plastic and landing face down in pile of squeaky pink unicorns.

I can see Mike standing in the doorway, talking to Dad like I knew he would be. Dad's slapping Mike on the back like they're old friends, which, they are—if your best friend lies to you behind your back about all the pot he smokes when you're not looking.

My dad turns around. "Joe, Mike's here!"

I survive the toy obstacle course and meet them at the door. Mike and I give each other the fist bump.

Dad is beaming, still clapping Mike on the back. "Did you know Mike got early acceptance into M.I.T?"

I knew months ago. Seriously old news.

"Yup, dude's a mad scientist," I say, trying hard not to laugh. And trying hard not to be jealous. I swear my folks would adopt Mike if they could.

"What are you guys up to tonight?" Dad's making annoying

small talk, even though he already knows I'm on Ruby-duty. I make a face that says, *Don't you know you I'm baby-sitting your lovely second child?*

Just then the girl in question screams through the living room, voice pitched at brain-shattering decibels as she pushes past me, attaching herself to Mike's leg like the face-hugger from Alien. Three-year-olds can be monsters. Every time Ruby screeches, I want to buy my dad a fresh pack of condoms. You've gotta catch the little swimmers before they mutate into something dangerous.

"What's up, little sis?" Mike scratches Ruby's messy blonde head with his knuckles, smiling like he really loves kids.

She bellows something that doesn't even sound human and tears away from Mike's leg, running off in the other direction. I hear toys being thrown behind us. Big toys that do damage when they hit something. It's going to be a long night.

"You like pizza?" Dad asks Mike, as though the kid has never had pizza in the five million years he's been coming over. It takes every ounce of my strength not to roll my eyes.

"I love pizza, Mr. Bloedel," Mike says, giving me *the look*. The one that says, *I've got your stuff.*

You know. The stuff.

The happy stuff.

The stuff that makes you feel like you're floating in a warm bath of dreams, high in the sky, where nothing can bring you down. The stuff that makes you forget that the whole world sucks and everyone thinks you're a loser. I smile in spite of myself, thinking about what Mike has in his backpack. Maybe it's going to be a good night after all.

THANK YOU!

Thank you *so much* for taking the time to read this book. If you've got a spare minute or two, please tell your friends about it, or go online and write a short review. I'd be forever grateful.

I love connecting with new people. Feel free to get social with me on Facebook, Twitter, or Google+. For news of future releases, you can also sign up for my email newsletter at www.ggsilverman.com. See you online!

ABOUT THE AUTHOR

G.G. Silverman lives north of Seattle with her husband and dog, both of whom are ridiculously adorable. When she isn't writing, she loves to explore the mossy woods and wind-swept coast of the Pacific Northwest, which provide moody inspiration for all her stories. She also enjoys bouts of inappropriate laughter, and hates wind chimes because they remind her of horror movies. To learn more about G.G., please visit her website at www.ggsilverman.com.

ACKNOWLEDGEMENTS

This book began as a voice in my ear one day as I was walking my dog Bananas, who used to growl at anyone who walked with a limp or shuffle. That day, the monologue that became the first page of this book came out of nowhere, and I rushed home and wrote it down. I then showed it to my writing group, who agreed it was the strongest thing I had written to date, and that gave me the courage to take it and make it into something more.

I spent the next year writing a first draft—the first book manuscript I had ever taken to completion and felt was representative of my true voice—then spent the next two years revising. Along the way, various people gave me the gift of truth—telling me what exactly wasn't working. Those people were publishing industry pros and fellow writing workshop attendees, from places like the Big Sur Children's Writing Workshop, the Oregon Coast Children's Book Writers Workshop (OCCBWW), the SCBWI NY Winter Conference, and especially LitReactor's YA workshop, where rockstar classmates Melissa Barlow, Lauren Spieller, and Laura M. Kolar gave me very useful suggestions. My critique group, comprised of awesome fellow YA writers Carly Hilios and Adam Taylor, also deserves a huge pat on the back for patiently wading through and commenting on several broken drafts on the way to this one. Beta readers were instrumental through the revision process as well—folks like Ross Kramer, Dr. Therese Huston, Jonathan Eric Foster, and YA librarian/author Danielle Dreger all generously gave their time and shared their thoughts. Thanks also to firearms expert John Hays for teaching me how to shoot, and for bulletproofing (pun intended) the firearms usage references in my story. Brianna Young, my office assistant while this book was being written, gets kudos for researching so many little details that helped shape the story. And a very big thanks to my editor Devin C. Griffiths, a phenomenal writer in his own right, who always saw my potential and knew I had it in me to pull through.

When you're writing a book, having people cheer you on is everything. This is where I tip my hat to my husband, family, and to all my friends, both online and off: you believed in me, and gave me the support to make my dream of publishing a book come true. I couldn't have done this without you.

CPSIA information can be obtained
at www.ICGtesting.com
Printed in the USA
LVOW13s2359190717
541968LV00009B/162/P

Successful Parties
and
How To Give Them